# you're
# bacon me
## crazy

## Also by Suzanne Nelson

*Cake Pop Crush*

*Macarons at Midnight*

*Hot Cocoa Hearts*

*Serendipity's Footsteps*

# you're bacon me crazy

### suzanne nelson

SCHOLASTIC INC.

For my bacon-crazed brothers,
Bobby, Clay, Brad, and Steve, with love.

Copyright © 2014 by Suzanne Nelson
Bacon illustration © Memphisslim/Shutterstock, Inc.

All rights reserved. Published by Scholastic Inc., *Publishers since 1920.* SCHOLASTIC and associated logos are trademarks and/or registered trademarks of Scholastic Inc.

The publisher does not have any control over and does not assume any responsibility for author or third-party websites or their content.

This book is a work of fiction. Names, characters, places, and incidents are either the product of the author's imagination or are used fictitiously, and any resemblance to actual persons, living or dead, business establishments, events, or locales is entirely coincidental.

ISBN 978-1-338-09919-5

10 9 8 7 6 5 4 3 2         17 18 19 20

Printed in the U.S.A.         40
First printing 2016

Book design by Jennifer Rinaldi and Yaffa Jaskoll

# chapter
## one

I could practically taste my new creation already. Lightly toasted bread spread with goat cheese, topped with arugula and diced chicken, and sprinkled with bacon bits for a crunchy finish. My fingertips tingled impatiently. I was eager to start stacking my ingredients into the perfect sandwich. This was how I always got toward the end of the school day, when all I could think about was getting to Aunt Cleo's Tasty Truck.

Of course, I didn't see the last step on the hallway stairs. And of course, it was my best friend, Mei Kwan, who rescued me. She grabbed my arm just before I fell head over heels into the throng of kids surging toward the door.

"Tessa!" Mei sighed and gave me the scolding smile she's perfected over our ten years of friendship. "No daydreaming until we're in the trample-free zone."

I blinked, shaking my visions of sandwiches out of my head. "Sorry." I shrugged, laughing. "You know I can't interrupt inspiration. When the food muse strikes, I must obey."

Together, Mei and I swept out the door into a cool mist tinged with sunlight. The sounds of the city — car horns and cable cars and the bustle of people — carried over to us on the wind. This time of year in San Francisco, the sun is constantly fighting with fog for attention. This afternoon, it seemed like the sun might stand a chance.

"You need to tell your food muse to stop talking to you during school," Mei quipped, then stopped, glancing at my hair. "Hey, have you done a bobby-pin check lately? You're still wearing three."

"Oh no." I touched the three rhinestone bobby pins in my curly black hair. Each pin stood for something important I was supposed to remember. When I remembered to do the important thing, I took out the bobby pin. This morning I'd started out with three bobby pins. Now I still had three, and I couldn't even remember what they were supposed to *help* me remember!

I began ticking off things I had done right today. "I turned in all my homework, I remembered my gym sneakers. . . ." I gave Mei a *help me* look.

"What about for tomorrow?" Mei asked.

"My spelling list!" I smacked my forehead and a curl sprang from my ponytail. I spun on my heel and jogged toward the school doors, calling over my shoulder, "Be right back!"

My aunt Cleo says great cooking minds can't help forgetting things like homework when they're creating culinary master-pieces. Too bad my teachers and parents don't agree. Neither does Mei. My best friend is so organized she color-coordinates her nail polish with her outfits . . . *every day*.

Back outside, I held up the spelling list to Mei, smiling trium-phantly. I slid a bobby pin out of my hair and into the front pocket of my overalls. "Bobby pin number one . . . gone!"

"Shhh." Mei's eyes were glued to something over my shoulder. "Check it out. Drama . . . stage right."

I tried to remember which direction stage right was. Mei is in the Theater Club. She speaks Shakespeare; I speak sandwich. It's a testimony to our friendship that we make it work.

I finally gave up and followed her gaze. Leaning against the low brick wall outside the entrance were three of Bayview Middle School's "Beautiful People."

You know the type: When they walked down the hallways, they parted the underling waters. The three we were looking at today were Tristan Maloney, Asher Rivers, and Karrie Lopes. Karrie, with her perfectly sleek, long brown hair, was a goddess with a dark side, striking awe and a certain level of fear into all the girls at Bayview. With one perfectly timed whisper, she could send anyone into social exile.

I didn't know Tristan or Asher very well; they were both stars of the school baseball team. Tristan was blond and blue-eyed, and actually seemed pretty friendly. As for Asher . . . Well, last year he'd had his birthday party at a fancy hotel, complete with a live band, and I'd heard him call it "subpar." If that wasn't the mark of an overprivileged, grade-A pretty boy, I didn't know what was. Still, he was gorgeous, no doubt about it. I'd never seen his cappuccino skin with so much as one zit, and his chocolate hair broke in wavy, swept-back curls that anyone would envy.

But right now, Asher's usually flawless cool was cratering into a look of surprised annoyance. Marching toward him, wearing a Burberry raincoat and a frighteningly volcanic expression, was his mom.

"Asher Rivers, you're grounded," Mrs. Rivers was barking at her son, "and that's only the beginning. . . ." She latched on to Asher's arm and steered him down the sidewalk toward her car, which was parked illegally, hazards blinking, blocking one entire lane of traffic. Over the blaring horns of unhappy commuters, Mrs. Rivers's voice could be heard launching into a tirade about how money doesn't just fall from the sky.

I felt a tickle of curiosity as I watched Mrs. Rivers all but shove Asher into the car. And I noticed Asher throw a wink at Tristan and Karrie over his shoulder, as if none of this was a big deal.

There was a single beat of silence as Asher's car disappeared into the stream of traffic, then Tristan laughed out a low "Busted," and everyone else burst into excited whispers.

"Wow," Mei said. "I'm glad you forgot your spelling list. It was worth waiting to see that."

"Did you see that smug look on his face?" I shook my head. "Whatever he did, he didn't seem to care."

"He lives in a penthouse suite in the Presidio and has a country estate in Napa," Mei said. "How bad can his punishment be?" She sighed. "I want his life."

"I don't," I said sincerely. "It might mean trading in my spatula for stilettos. Ugh."

Mei laughed, then checked her watch. "Ooh, we should get going," she said. "I really want to stop by Vanity's."

She was already a step ahead of me on the sidewalk, weaving through the groups of still-lingering kids. Some of them waited to catch a ride home on the Powell/Hyde cable cars, and others got picked up by parents. Mei and I both lived only about three blocks away, but it had taken years for our parents to agree to let us walk instead of picking us up. We finally got the go-ahead last fall, and now we walk whenever we can.

As we turned onto Hyde Street, the bay, dotted with tiny white boats, stretched out before us in brilliant blue. Russian Hill is one of the oldest neighborhoods in San Francisco, and even though it's only one of the forty-four hills in the sprawling city, I think it's the best. Pastel-colored town houses stand shoulder-to-shoulder with bodegas, restaurants, and boutiques, giving every street a feeling of happy chaos. Far below us, down the street's steep hill, I could make out the Tasty Truck sitting at the corner of Lombard, shining silver in the sunlight. Just the sight of it made me smile.

We made a quick stop at Vanity's, Mei's favorite clothing store, so that she could scour the clearance rack. While she shopped, I texted Cleo my new sandwich idea. As soon as the salesclerk handed Mei her shopping bag, I was out the door, itching to get to the truck.

Mei, in the meantime, clutched her shopping bag over her heart, practically squealing with delight. I knew she was dying for me to ask, so I did what any best friend would do, and said, "So . . . show me what you got."

She lifted a pink, petally skirt out of the bag and held it up under her chin. "Don't you just love it? It's so Debbie Reynolds in *Singin' in the Rain*!" Mei is obsessed with movie musicals; she's streamed them all on her mom's iPad.

I laughed, shaking my head. "Another pink skirt? Really? Your entire wardrobe is pink."

She sniffed indignantly. "My wardrobe isn't simply 'pink.' It's fuchsia, rose, champagne, bubble gum . . ."

"Pink, pink, pink," I sang, until she playfully slapped my arm.

"Speaking of pink skirts," she said, "where is the one I got *you* for Christmas?"

I opened my mouth, then closed it again.

Mei's dark eyes flashed. "Don't tell me you lost it already."

"It's not lost. I think it just . . . took a vacation." This meant the skirt was buried in the pile of sweet, eyeletty clothing Mei kept giving me in the hopes that I'd transform into a girly fashionista. So far, the bottom of my closet looked adorable.

I shrugged as we waved to the tourists snapping photos from

a passing cable car. "Come on, Mei, you know I had to wear my lucky overalls on the first day back from winter break."

"Overalls." Mei tried her best to look stern, but she couldn't keep it up. "And what about your New Year's resolution to get contacts?"

"Um, I believe that was *your* New Year's resolution to *convince* me to get contacts." I gave my lime-green-framed glasses an affectionate tap. "You keep trying extreme makeovers, and I keep saying no."

"You're hopeless, Tessa Kostas!" Mei giggled, but there was a determined look in her eyes. I hoped she wouldn't launch into her patented *learn-to-love-lip-gloss* lecture. "And don't give me that excuse about fashion and food not mixing. Look at your aunt."

She pointed toward the Tasty Truck, which was only a few feet away. Sure enough, there was Cleo, leaning out the window. She wore a blue-and-green-printed romper, hoop earrings, and a batik scarf tied around her chestnut hair. My aunt *did* dress cooler than me, but I was okay with that, because Cleo's never really fit neatly into the whole "aunt" package. She's my dad's sister, but she's half my dad's age. At twenty-three, she's only ten years older than me. So even though she's an aunt, she feels like the closest I'll ever get to a big sister.

"Greetings, school-goers!" Cleo called to me and Mei. "Come see the new menu!" she added excitedly, jumping out of the truck. Cleo's boyfriend, Gabe, who runs the truck with her, was sliding a colorful menu into a slot on the truck's side.

As I read, a smile spread across my face:

### bacon me crazy blt
Crisp seasoned bacon, roasted tomatoes, baby romaine
& Cleo's special sauce on toasted eight-grain bread

### fan me bánh mì
Spicy grilled chicken, cucumber, cilantro, pickled carrots
& hot chili sauce on a baguette

### grilled brieze
Smoked brie, avocado & herb bouquet
on grilled pumpernickel

### gobble me up
Cajun-fried turkey, cran-apple rémoulade
& stuffing on corn bread

### the greatest gatsby
Shredded masala beef, sweet potato fries
& mango chutney on French bread

### the chic greek
Smashed chickpeas, kalamata olives, red onion, cherry
tomatoes & feta cheese on pita bread

### desserts
Almond cupcake
Carrot-cake donut

"You used the sandwich names I came up with!" I hugged Cleo, beaming. I'd been brainstorming for the menu revamp over the holiday break, and now the names were up on the board for the world to see.

"It looks great!" Mei said. "*And* it makes me hungry."

"Then it's already working!" Cleo said. "And I like the new sandwich recipe you texted me, Tessa. You'll have to help me come up with a few more, now that we're going to" — Gabe did a drumroll on the side of the truck, and Cleo flung her arms wide and cried — "Flavorfest!"

I whooped as my aunt did a celebratory dance. "You mean we actually got invited?" I asked, feeling a surge of joy.

Cleo waved a letter at me. "I just got it today!" She grinned like a cat who'd swallowed a whole flock of canaries.

Flavorfest is the food-truck competition that the city holds every year, but it's by invitation only. Hundreds of people, along with San Fran's top food critics, come to the fair to sample the city's best food-truck cuisine. A bad showing at the fair could end the life of a food truck, but a great one could secure it a permanent place on the map. Signor Antonio, the owner of Gelatta Love, the gelato truck parked one block down from us, is at Flavorfest every year. As a result, his gelato is so famous that people come from all over the country just to taste it.

It had taken three long years without invites, but now, finally, the Tasty Truck had made the cut. "When's the fair?" I asked.

"February eighth," Cleo said. "And that's not all. The Bacon Me Crazy BLT is one of the nominees for the Flavorfest Best Award."

"Yum!" Mei said. "That's always been my favorite sandwich."

"Mine, too, and it's all in Cleo's special sauce," Gabe said, giving Cleo a sweet peck on the cheek.

It was true. Cleo kept the ingredients for her BLT sauce so secret that no one knew what was in it, not even Gabe and me. When I bit into one of her BLTs, I tasted faint whispers of avocado and mayo, and a hint of mustard, but I could never figure out the rest. Whatever it was, the sauce was a mouthwatering masterpiece. It was my dream that someday I'd be able to cook up something as special as that sauce, too. That someday, I might be as good a cook as Cleo.

Cleo rubbed her hands together. "We only have about a month to get ready, so we've got a lot of work to do."

Suddenly, I felt a flash of inspiration. "Hey!" I cried, grabbing Cleo's arm. "Maybe we could do a line of bacon desserts and bacon sides, to complement the BLT. Maybe bacon-bits brownies, or bacon fudge?"

"Talk about bacon overload." Mei giggled.

"There's no such thing," I said indignantly. "Even if you don't eat bacon, you want what it gives you. That cozy, home-cooked, warm-blanket feeling. We cook that feeling into food, and nobody can get enough of it."

"Well, considering how much Tessa daydreams about food, I think she's got you covered in the new-recipe department," Mei said to Cleo. "She almost broke her neck thinking up that sandwich she texted you about."

Cleo laughed. "Were you thinking about sandwiches this morning, too? You left your lunch on the front stoop on your way to school."

"I was wondering what happened to it! Bobby pin number two," I said, sliding another one into my pocket.

Suddenly, I spotted a wave of customers — including a bunch of kids from Bayview — heading down the hill, straight for our truck. We always had a crazy post-school rush at this hour, and it was time to get to work.

Mei gave me a quick hug and said she'd be window-shopping right nearby. I turned and entered the delicious-smelling interior of the truck with Cleo and Gabe. Then I pulled on my apron, and we each took our positions at our stations. I was manning orders, Gabe was dicing and stocking fresh veggies, and Cleo was putting together the sandwiches. We'd switch off positions throughout the afternoon, depending on how busy things got.

Nick Lee, who I knew from math class, came up to the truck window and ordered a Grilled Brieze. His girlfriend, Liz Abbott, wanted a Gobble Me Up. Next in line was another classmate of mine, Ben Warner, who always ordered the BLT.

"Here you go." I handed Ben the wrapped sandwich through the window. "With extra sauce."

Ben's freckled face lit up. "Thanks, Tessa. You always remember." He craned his neck, looking suddenly sheepish. "Hey . . . is Mei around? We were supposed to meet here after school."

*They were?* Before I could ask Ben to clarify, Mei appeared, her cheeks blazing pink. "I'm here!" she blurted.

I stared at her for a second, wondering exactly what was going on. Mei and I had known Ben since elementary school, and usually Mei was busy faux-gagging at Ben's gross armpit squelches, or slapping his hand away when he tried to snag one of her mom's homemade dumplings from her during lunch. I'd never seen her blush around him before.

"Um, we're going to go," Mei said haltingly to me. "I promised Mom I'd babysit the twins tonight so she could go to Dad's cello concert, and Ben said he'd help." She snuck an under-the-eyelashes glance at Ben, and they both smiled.

"Oh," I said, which was just about the only syllable I could eke out in my shock. Ben was going to help Mei *babysit*? That wasn't just odd; that was epic. Now it was my turn to blush, because suddenly I felt awkward, like I was throwing everyone off balance just by being there. "Okay," I finally managed, "well, I'll call you later."

"Sure," Mei said, but it was more like an afterthought, because she was already walking away with Ben, ducking her head in a shy way that looked suspiciously like flirting.

My eyes lingered on Mei and Ben as I tried to puzzle through what had just happened. But a group of camera-wielding tourists had lined up at the window, and I had to focus on work.

Cleo suggested we switch positions, so this time she shouted the orders back to me while I made sandwiches. My fingers flew, slicing bread, dipping into the containers of diced chicken and avocado slices, watching my ingredients stack higher and higher.

The Tasty Truck is basically my happy place. From the first time I stepped inside three years ago, I fell in love. The steel counters, cabinets, and cooktops are sleek and shiny, and the fridge is always stocked. Some people get claustrophobic in food trucks. But to me, it's a cozy nest filled with mouthwatering food, buzzing energy, and inspiration.

Before Cleo and Gabe opened the truck, most days I came home from school to a nanny. Mom and Dad both work in finance, and sometimes it feels like they're away more than they're home. Dad was in Zurich last month, and now they're both in Rome. Neither my parents nor the nannies cared much for my "kitchen experiments," which is what I called my cooking when I was younger. But then Cleo moved into the upstairs "nanny quarters" of our town house. My dad made a deal with her that she could stay there while she got her truck business up and running, as long as she helped keep an eye on me, too. Cleo and I got busy turning the rooftop of our house into an amazing organic garden, where she gets all the fresh veggies and herbs for the truck. Cleo never scolded me for messes in the kitchen. Instead, she helped me make them. And suddenly, life didn't seem quite so lonely. Especially on a day like today, when the Tasty Truck was hopping with customers and Cleo, Gabe, and I were in our groove.

The line finally tapered off around 4:45, which was perfect, because we usually close around five. We were counting the register and locking the food away in the storage cabinets when I heard a little cough outside the truck.

I spun around and glanced out the window, startled to spot Mrs. Rivers standing there, still in her Burberry raincoat. I'd never seen Asher's mom at the truck before!

"Um, would you like to order a sandwich?" I asked clumsily.

"No, thank you," she said politely. She gave me a small smile, then added, "Tessa Kostas, right?" I nodded, surprised that she knew my name; she must have remembered me from Asher's birthday bash last year. "May I please speak to the owner of the truck?" she asked.

"Sure," I said, feeling a little nervous as I turned to summon Cleo. I wondered if there was some sort of complaint coming.

Cleo hurried over to the window, and I pretended to be wiping off the counter while I eavesdropped.

"I have a bit of an odd request," I heard Mrs. Rivers say after she and Cleo had introduced themselves. "I wanted to talk to you about my son, Asher. He and Tessa go to school together." She paused, as if the next words were difficult to say. "He needs an after-school job, and I thought this would be a good place for him to work. I was wondering if you needed help."

"Asher wants to work at *our* truck?" I blurted, before I could stop myself. Cleo and Mrs. Rivers both glanced at me, surprised.

Then Mrs. Rivers shook her head. "Not exactly, but he doesn't have a choice. It's part of a punishment I'm giving him, a lesson in learning to appreciate things a bit more."

Suddenly, I remembered how Mrs. Rivers had scolded Asher outside the school earlier that afternoon. Having Asher work here was probably the fallout from that. But there was no way Cleo was going to hire Asher. The truck was a tight fit for three people, let alone four.

But then, Cleo shocked me by saying, "Actually, Gabe and I were just talking about hiring more help for the next few months."

They were? I swallowed, and my heart hammered.

"This will work out perfectly," Cleo continued. "When can Asher start?"

"After school tomorrow," Mrs. Rivers said. She extended a hand to Cleo. "Thank you so much. Asher's had a rough year, and I think this will be a wonderful change, and challenge, for him."

Gabe nodded. "We'll be glad to have him."

Mrs. Rivers nodded once more, gratefully, and then hurried off toward her parked car.

The second she was gone, I spun to Cleo, a steady dread simmering in my veins. "But . . . but Asher can't work here!" I sputtered. I quickly painted a picture of his personality for my aunt, hoping the birthday-party story would discourage her. Then I added, "There's not enough room in the truck for four of us, and I'm sure he doesn't know a thing about cooking or food, and we have so much to do to get ready for Flavorfest already. . . ." *And he'll ruin everything,* I almost said, but didn't.

Cleo smiled. "It'll be fine," she said as she finished buckling the veggie containers into their seat belts for the ride home. "Like

I told Mrs. Rivers, Gabe and I were talking about hiring some extra help anyway."

Gabe nodded while he locked the cabinets so nothing would fly open. "I'm going to be busy working on my grad thesis for the next couple of months, and there's an evening horticulture class Cleo wants to take at Berkeley."

"Besides," Cleo added, "having Asher around will give us *more* time to work on our Flavorfest menu."

Doubt must have been all over my face, because Cleo laughed and tweaked my nose playfully. "Come on, Tessa. Just cut him some slack, and I'm sure your cooking instincts will rub off on him in no time. Okay?"

I sighed, but because I love Cleo and didn't want to argue with her, I reluctantly bit into the inevitable. "Okay," I said. "But if he gives all of our customers botulism, don't blame me."

Cleo laughed so hard she snorted, which is one of the things I love best about her. "Done," she finally said.

Cleo's reassurance didn't help, though. I was sure of one thing: There were about to be *way* too many cooks in the Tasty Truck kitchen.

# chapter
## two

"I can't believe you're complaining about having to work with Asher," Mei said the next morning before class. She grabbed her art history book, fluffed up her new pink skirt, then slammed her locker shut. "You know every other girl in school would die to be that close to him."

"*I'm* not every other girl," I said. "And cuteness doesn't count when he's so full of himself."

Just then, my cell phone buzzed. I checked the screen, then grabbed Mei's arm and whooped. "Look!" I showed her the

Facebook notification. "The Great Pillow Fight! It's our first blast about it!"

"That's . . . great," Mei said, but her voice turned reedy at the end, like she might be trying for more excitement than she felt.

"It's *fantastic*!" I corrected her. The Great Pillow Fight was my favorite San Fran tradition. Every year on Valentine's Day, more than a thousand people pack into Justin Herman Plaza with their pillows. When the Ferry Building clock tower strikes six P.M., you beat the tar out of everyone you can with your pillow. Cleo and Gabe took me to my first pillow fight when I was nine, and for the last four years, Mei and I have gone with them. "Last year was so much fun, remember? All those feathers stuck to your lips . . . hilarious."

"*Not* so hilarious." Mei flipped her shiny black hair indignantly. "I was picking goose down out of my mouth for hours."

I laughed. "Well, you're the one who insisted on wearing lip gloss."

"Of course I did," Mei said. She raised an arm like she was

preparing to recite Shakespeare. "To gloss or not to gloss . . . there's not *ever* a question."

I laughed. "Then maybe try a nonstick gloss for the fight this year."

I expected Mei to laugh, but instead she dropped her eyes. I felt a funny twinge in my stomach. "Tessa," Mei said quietly, "I've been thinking about Valentine's Day, and maybe we can try something —"

"Hey there, Pretty-in-Pink!" Ben interrupted, walking up to us.

"Hey," Mei said, giving him a smile. "I can't believe you noticed!" She swiveled slightly, making her skirt twirl.

"Sure I did," he said. "It looks nice."

I couldn't believe it. "Oh, come on, Ben." I laughed, ribbing him good-naturedly. "You spend more time making gum sculptures in class than paying attention. Since when do you notice things like clothes?"

He shrugged, but continued to smile goofily at Mei. "So . . . my mom's driving me to Vinyl after school to see if they have any new Rolling Stones LPs, if you guys want to come along?" I got the distinct impression that even though the invite included both of us, it was *meant* for Mei.

"That sounds great!" Mei said. "I can see if they have Yul Brynner's *The King and I*. We're putting it on in May, and I'm going to be Anna."

I was about to say that I wouldn't be able to come with them, but then the bell rang, and Ben and Mei were all smiles and waves saying good-bye to each other. Since it didn't even seem to matter that I was standing right next to them, I let it go.

Mei glanced over her shoulder at Ben as she and I walked to art history. "He looks different this semester, don't you think?" she asked. "Maybe it's his new haircut."

"Definitely," I said. "Bed head is so in right now."

Mei giggled. "I think it's kind of cute. And you should have seen him with the twins last night. He let them finger-paint his face *and* he changed a diaper. It was adorable."

"Wait a sec." I stopped in the doorway and studied Mei's face. "You realize you just described Ben as 'cute' *and* 'adorable.' Are — are you crushing on him?"

"I don't know." Mei shrugged, but then she smiled dreamily. "Maybe."

"Wow," I said quietly, my heart diving to my toes. I tried to smile enthusiastically, but it didn't quite work. Luckily, though, Mei was still in her Ben haze and didn't catch on.

The final bell rang and we took our seats as Mr. Toulouse gave the morning announcements.

"Today we're going to be discussing your upcoming artist projects," he said. "You'll be partnering up to study an artist of your choice. You'll research the artist, and then you and your partner will put together a presentation for the class on what you discovered."

Mei and I gave each other silent nods, which meant partnering up was a no-brainer. But as Mr. Toulouse droned on, I found it hard to concentrate. The new semester had only started yesterday, but suddenly Mei was "in like" with a boy who used to put glue in our hair in kindergarten. Neither one of us had ever even had a boyfriend before. My life was starting to feel slightly disorienting, like being in someone else's kitchen and having no idea where anything was. This was all new territory, and I was going to be finding my way blind.

When I got to the Tasty Truck that afternoon, Asher was nowhere to be seen.

"I knew it," I said, slipping my apron over my head. "He's a no-show."

"He'll be here," Cleo said. "Mrs. Rivers will make sure of it." She tossed some diced chicken on the grill, then handed me a bunch of fresh cilantro. "Can you chop this while we wait?"

Normally, Gabe does the chopping, but he had to attend a grad seminar that afternoon. So I nodded and got to work, and before long, I'd forgotten all about Asher, and even about Mei and Ben. The tangy, greeny scent of cilantro wafted pleasantly from the cutting board, and my hands found their easy rhythm. I got so absorbed in my work that I didn't even notice at first when Signor Antonio stuck his weathered face through the window of the truck.

"*Buongiorno, signorine,*" he said, tipping his fedora. He frowned and added, "I come bearing tragic news."

I felt a tremor of worry, and then Signor Antonio slapped a newspaper down on the window ledge. He jabbed a finger at the headline. "It's the Flavorfest. It's *rovinato*! Ruined!"

Cleo and I gasped in unison, and I grabbed the paper. The headline read: RESTAURANT TYCOON PANS FLAVORFEST IN FAVOR OF FINE DINING.

"This Mr. Morgan," Signor Antonio sputtered. "He owns a dozen five-star restaurants around the city. He plans to show them off at a Taste of San Fran Fine Food Festival, but he wants it to take the place of Flavorfest. He wants to kill Flavorfest!"

Cleo frowned as she read the article. "He wants to hold the fine-food tasting on Folsom Street, where we have Flavorfest every year," she told us, her forehead creasing. "And he wants to have it on the same day."

"So, the restaurants and food trucks do Flavorfest together," I said. "That's an easy problem to solve."

"Mr. Morgan doesn't think so," Cleo murmured, still reading. "He says there's not enough room for the trucks and the restaurant booths. So only restaurants will be invited to the Taste of San Fran. No food trucks will be allowed, and Flavorfest will have to find a new venue for that Saturday, or get canceled altogether."

"What?" I cried, my stomach sinking. "He can't do that! People from all over the city come to Flavorfest."

"I don't know," said Cleo, sounding uncertain. "Mr. Morgan is like the Donald Trump of restaurants in this city. He's got a lot of pull."

Signor Antonio threw up his hands. "Flavorfest is *finito*!" he cried with gusto, then turned down the sidewalk. "No more gelato today. I'm going home to pack for Tuscany."

"Oh boy," Cleo whispered to me. "I'll be back when I change his mind." Then she hurried out, slipping a comforting arm around Signor Antonio's ancient stooped shoulders as she walked him back to his truck.

I read through the rest of the article, and by the time the truck door swung open again, my mood had gone from sizzled to scorched.

"I cannot believe the nerve of this jerk!" I hollered, just before turning to see Asher in the doorway.

Asher raised an eyebrow at me. "Geez, I know I'm late already," he grumbled. "You don't have to yell at me."

"Sorry," I said, feeling my face get hot as I mentally kicked myself. "I didn't mean you."

Asher stepped all the way inside the truck. Up close, his pillowy lips and cinnamon eyes made it hard not to stare, and he smelled faintly of coconut, like a perfect day at the beach. I didn't want to be affected by being this close to him, but my senses overruled my common sense.

"Um, you *are* late, though," I mumbled, attempting to recover before he caught on.

"Yeah, well, it doesn't really matter." He glanced around, looking displeased. "Man, this is tighter than a cell at Alcatraz. How can you possibly move in here?"

"Oh, we manage," I said coolly. He'd been inside the truck for all of fifteen seconds and he was already insulting it?

"Asher!" Cleo said, reentering the truck. "Welcome." She glanced at me, trying to take a mood reading. She must've come to the conclusion that the new employee and I weren't in danger of strangling each other (at least, not yet), because she added, "I need to run back to the house to get a few things from the garden." Then a flash of concern crossed her face. "I'm also going to make a few phone calls to other food truckers, just to see if I can find out more about what's happening with Flavorfest."

I nodded. All the food truckers in our part of the city knew one another, and they'd formed an unspoken alliance, trying not to serve competing foods and throwing business one another's way whenever they could. Cleo says it's the best way for food trucks to survive: by sticking together.

"Tessa, you get Asher started, and I'll be back soon." She gave us a wave, and then she was gone, leaving me and Asher alone.

"I want to set the record straight." Asher leaned against the counter, arms folded. "I don't really want to be here, but I don't have a choice."

"So why are you here?" I demanded, crossing my arms over my chest as well.

"I was tossing a ball around with some friends at my mom's house and broke a vase." He shrugged. "She wants me to pay for another one."

"And you don't think you should have to," I said matter-of-factly.

His amber eyes flashed angrily. "She has a ton of vases. One doesn't matter."

"Maybe it does to her," I snapped. Did he have any idea how spoiled he sounded right now?

Clearly he didn't, because he gave a disgruntled sigh and added, "Just don't expect me to be the smiley 'Can I take your order?' guy, okay?"

I couldn't believe anyone could be so obnoxious, and I wanted more than anything to wipe that proud look right off his fine face. But I figured I'd take the high road. Cleo would want me to. "Okay," I managed to say through gritted teeth. "So if customer service isn't your thing, then you can be the garde-manger, our pantry chef. You'll restock ingredients as we need them, and you'll buckle up all the food and cabinets before we move the truck at the end of the day. It's really important so things don't go flying." I showed him where the belts were in the cabinets for strapping down the food containers. "Oh, and you'll be in charge of the cold line, too."

In response to his blank look, I added, "The cold line is the area where we prep all of our cold ingredients, like our fresh veggies and herbs." I pointed to a two-foot countertop that had stainless-steel containers of tomatoes, peppers, and herbs lined up. "I can show you some of the basics," I said, picking up a knife. "We can start with mincing and work up to julienning. . . ."

"Whatever," Asher said, rolling his eyes. "Isn't it all the same, anyway? Chopping up a bunch of rabbit food?"

I clenched my teeth again. Rabbit food? Seriously? I tried to channel calmness with deep breathing, something Cleo had been trying (and failing) to teach me. But then I glanced out the window and saw the regular horde of after-school customers marching down the hill. And any calmness coming my way swiftly vanished.

"Call it whatever you want," I said briskly, "Just . . . try cutting some of it up, okay? Please?"

I didn't wait for him to answer. Instead, I whirled to the window and began taking orders. For the first few minutes, I held my own, filling the orders with the fresh diced veggies and meat we'd already prepped. But when I started running low on some of the cold ingredients, things started to get ugly. I glanced at Asher and saw him carelessly mutilating a poor onion and tossing it, flaky skin and all, into one of the steel containers. On the cutting board were the sorry remains of three pulverized tomatoes and a pile of cut carrots that looked like jigsaw pieces.

"Here," I said, swiftly stepping in front of him, "just let me take over for a second. We're getting completely backed up out there."

"Fine by me," he said, moving out of the way.

My fingers flew as I minced and diced and restocked the cold containers. "Can you please toast some eight-grain bread?" I asked, thinking that toast was something he couldn't possibly mess up. "I've got four orders of BLTs to fill."

He shrugged grudgingly, then popped a couple of pieces of bread in the toaster. Two minutes later, he handed them back to me, charred. "I guess I left them in too long," he said indifferently.

I blew out a frustrated breath, then grabbed new slices of bread and muttered, "Never mind. I'll do it myself."

I knew that Asher would be a disaster.

I finally handed off the four BLTs to Nick, Liz, and some friends of theirs. Then I felt a jolt of shock when I saw that Tristan and Karrie were next in line. This was the first time any Beautiful People had ever graced our truck with their presence. From the sour look on Karrie's face, I guessed that this visit hadn't been her idea.

"Hey, Tessa," Tristan said with a smile, as if it were the norm for us to talk all the time. I'd heard Ben say once that Tristan was pretty grounded, not stuck up like some of the other Beautiful People. But this was the first time I'd witnessed it, and it made me drop my guard enough to smile and say hi back. "I've heard about your famous BLT, so I thought I'd give it a try," he added. "And" — he stuck his head in through the window — "offer some moral support to my bud here. Hang in there, Ash. Your first day's almost over."

"Yeah, yeah," Asher mumbled, tossing a hand towel toward Tristan. But Tristan had managed to get a weak smile out of Asher, which was more than I'd seen so far. "Hey," Asher said to me, "I'm going to take my break now. I'll be back in a few. . . ."

"What?" I stared at him. "This is our busiest time of day! You can't take a break!"

He scowled. "Your aunt can take a few bucks from my paycheck for it. No biggie." And before I could utter another word, he had brushed passed me and was outside, chatting with Karrie. The second Tristan joined them with his freshly made BLT, Karrie glanced at the sandwich and grimaced.

"Omigod." She put a hand over her mouth as if to keep what she was saying secret, but still spoke loudly enough so I could hear, "You're not going to eat that, are you? That truck probably breaks every health code in the book."

I felt my blood boil. The girl did *not* know what she was talking about.

Tristan only grinned at her, then took an enormous bite. "Mmmm . . . delicious."

Karrie's laugh was like shattering glass. Way too harsh. "You can't be serious," she said, then she laid her hand on Asher's arm, like she was staking out her territory. "What are you doing, Ash? You don't belong here."

"I know," Asher mumbled. "Talk about cruel and unusual punishment."

"Well, at least you don't smell like bacon grease . . . yet," she said, then laughed like that was the funniest joke in the world.

"Hey, I *love* that smell," Tristan said, elbowing Asher. Then he turned to Karrie. "Come on, let's let Ash get back to work." He waved good-naturedly at me. "See you later, Tessa! Thanks for the great eats!"

I smiled tightly and waved back, but only for Tristan's benefit. The second Asher reluctantly stepped back into the truck, I turned away to avoid seeing the smug look on his face.

We worked in total silence for the next hour; or, I worked while Asher texted. The more he texted and refused to work, the more furious I got. When Cleo finally came back to the truck, my temper was burnt to a crisp.

"So . . . how was the first day on the job?" Cleo asked Asher with a smile.

Asher shrugged, and I could only mutter, "Can we just close up . . . *please*?"

Cleo gave me a questioning look, but nodded, and within ten minutes, we were ready. Asher sat up front with her for the ride back to the parking garage, and I took the third foldout seat in the back of the truck. We pulled out onto Hyde Street, and as we turned a corner, chaos struck.

I shrieked as one of the cabinets to my right flew open and a container of tomatoes flew out, landing upside down in my lap. The onions were airborne next, and then the masala beef. But the very last bump in the road was the one that did it — the one that dumped the entire container of Cleo's special sauce all over my head.

When Cleo opened the back of the truck, there I was in my seat, covered in congealed beef, thick rivulets of sauce oozing down my face.

Asher burst out laughing, and when I'd finally wiped my eyes enough to see, there was Cleo, doubled over in her snorty laugh stance.

"Asher," I managed to hiss, trying to wipe the goo off my face. "You were *supposed* to buckle everything down."

"Oh yeah," he said, trying to catch his breath between laughs. "I forgot about that." He shrugged as if it were no big deal that I was covered in slime. "Sorry."

That was it. The last straw.

"That's all you can say?" I cried, the rage I'd felt building up all afternoon exploding out of me. "You're not sorry. You're too conceited to be sorry!"

"Tessa —" Cleo started, but I cut her off.

"No, no, he barely worked at all today, and when he did, he ruined everything he touched."

"Well, you didn't exactly show me the ropes, did you?" Asher shot back.

"I tried, but you were on such a high horse you didn't listen!" I made a weak attempt to brush some sauce off my dripping overalls. "You think working in the truck is so beneath you. You said yourself it was cruel and unusual punishment!"

"So?" he said, his voice deepening in anger. "I never wanted to work here in the first place!" He threw up his hands. "You know what? I don't care what my mom says. I can't do this. I'll find another way to pay her back." He tossed his apron into the back of the truck and turned away. "I quit."

He marched out of the parking garage, leaving Cleo and me staring after him.

"I can't stand him." I seethed. "He's the most stuck-up, spoiled person I've ever met. . . ."

Cleo took one of her calming breaths. "He might need some time to adjust. It was only his first day."

"And thankfully his last," I said.

"I'm not so sure," Cleo said. "I doubt his mom's going to let him off the hook, and we really do need some more help with the truck." She smiled winningly at me, and I instantly shook my head, reading her mind.

"Oh no," I said. "No way."

"Just try talking to him at school tomorrow," Cleo pleaded. "Obviously you got off on the wrong foot, but if he comes back, you're going to have to find a way to work together. And if any-body can change his attitude about cooking, it's you. Please?"

Ugh. When she said *please* in her sweet, big-sisterly way, how could I possibly say no? "All right," I said grudgingly. "I'll *try*."

"Thank you, Tessa. You're the best." She smiled gratefully, then shook her head at the explosion of sauce inside the truck. "What a mess, huh?"

I nodded with a sigh. What a mess, indeed.

# chapter
# three

Three shampoos later, my hair was finally sauce-free, but I wasn't off the hook. Not even close. I walked into our kitchen, and there were Mom and Dad, fresh off the plane in their suits, two-peas-in-a-pinstripe.

"Sweetheart!" Mom hugged me. "We missed you!"

"You, too," I said. "How was Rome?"

Dad looked up from the pile of mail he was weeding through. "Conferences and boring business dinners." He went over to the stove and dipped a finger in the tomato sauce Cleo was making.

"Hands off, bro!" Cleo said, threatening to swat his hand with her wooden spoon, and he pulled away, laughing.

Dad flipped on the news in the den while Mom and I set the table. A minute later, Dad called us over to the TV.

"Did you know about this, Cleo?" he asked, pointing to the screen.

"We just found out about it today," Cleo said.

Bev Channing, the newscaster for Channel Seven, was talking about "The Flavorfest Controversy." Pictures of various food trucks from all over the city flashed across the screen. When I saw the Tasty Truck looking all shiny and bright, I squealed.

"It's a regular celebrity," Dad said.

We kept watching as Bev recapped what Signor Antonio had already told us. But then a man appeared on the screen wearing a svelte suit, smiling suavely.

"Mr. Morgan," Cleo whispered.

"I'm not trying to take anything away from the city," Mr. Morgan said smoothly. "San Francisco boasts some of the best restaurants in the country, and the Taste of San Fran festival will put our finest foods on display. Tourists come to our city for our restaurants and culture, not for our food trucks. Sure, food trucks give people quick and easy food choices, but those choices, I'm sad to say, aren't always healthy . . . or clean."

"What?" I shrieked.

"That's just despicable," Cleo said. "Doesn't he know we have to pass safety inspections and meet codes just like any restaurant does?"

"The fact is, food trucks aren't on par with our city's fine dining," Mr. Morgan was saying. "They're our fast-food options, but they don't belong at the Taste of San Fran."

Dad snapped off the TV. "Well, if I know Cleo," he said as we all sat down at the table, "she's putting together a battle plan. Am I right?"

Cleo nodded. "I talked to Gabe, and we're going to start a petition in the neighborhood to keep Flavorfest. If we make some noise, maybe the city council will ask Mr. Morgan to reschedule the Taste of San Fran."

"What about just moving Flavorfest to another location?" Dad asked.

"Gabe's looking into that with Signor Antonio, but there's a lot of red tape involved." Cleo took a bite of her pasta, then added, "I'm not giving up yet."

"Me either," I said, feeling newly determined. "We have all these new recipes that we're planning, and Cleo's BLT is going to win the Flavorfest Best Award this year. There's not a chance I'm going to let some high-powered suit ruin everything."

I swallowed thickly when Mom visibly stiffened at the word *suit*. I guess I didn't really blame her, either, considering she was sitting at our table wearing one.

"Well, even if Flavorfest does happen," Mom said, "I don't want you to get carried away, Tessa. I know if you had your way, you'd be in the kitchen every hour of the day, brewing up something or other."

"They're called recipes, Mom," I said, my voice hardening. I didn't add that recipes were something my mom never used, because she never cooked. She always said finance was her thing, not fricassee.

"No sarcasm, please, Tessa." She sighed. "How's your first

week back at school been so far? I hope you haven't been spending too many hours at the Tasty Truck. You know the rule. School comes first."

Mom just had to throw that comment in there . . . every time. When Cleo first opened the truck, Dad and I were gung ho about it, but Mom tried to talk Cleo out of it, encouraging her to get a "real job" instead (whatever that meant). Mom had never been enthused about my helping Cleo with the truck. But Dad said it was teaching me valuable "work ethic," so Mom let me do it. But not without reminding me regularly that other things, like homework, were more important.

"Tessa's been doing great with everything," Cleo said, winking at me. I smiled, grateful, as always, that she was there to put in a good word for me.

"All right," Mom said, and she turned back to me. "I just want you to keep a healthy balance between school, your friends, and cooking. Okay?"

A balance. I could not believe Mom was using that word with me. I wanted to tell her that she could balance better, too, and maybe spend less time traveling and more time at home. But then I looked at Cleo, and she shook her head slightly, meaning, *Don't go there.*

So, I took a deep breath. "Okay, Mom," I finally managed, and the rest of dinner went peacefully.

Back in my bedroom later, I lay awake for a long time, watching from my window as thick fog curled and tumbled over the Golden Gate Bridge. Just as I was finally getting drowsy, my door creaked open, and I saw Mom tiptoeing toward my bed. She slid under the covers with me and wrapped her arms around me, pressing her cold toes against mine. We laid there for a few minutes like that, which is something we haven't done since I was very young.

"You grow up a little more every time I go away," she whispered. "I wish I were here to see it happening." She kissed my forehead. "Love you."

"You, too," I whispered back as she slipped out of the room. Of course I loved my mom, but sometimes I felt like Cleo understood something about me that Mom just couldn't.

There was only one bobby pin tucked into my curls on Wednesday morning. It was there to make sure I didn't forget the unpleasant task ahead.

I got to school ten minutes early. Waiting at Asher's locker felt a little like trespassing on forbidden territory. My jittery nerves had me pacing and not knowing where to look.

No one at our school hangs out at the lockers of the Beautiful People unless you're one of them. But when Tristan caught sight of me as he came down the hallway with Asher, he didn't seem the least bit shocked. Asher, on the other hand, slowed down his pace, setting his jaw stubbornly like he was preparing for battle.

There was an awkward silence before Tristan broke the ice.

"Hey, Tessa," he said amicably. "So, things got off to a rough start yesterday, huh?"

I met Asher's gaze. There was no way I was going to give him the satisfaction of seeing me whining over what had happened. So I tossed my hair nonchalantly and said, "Actually, I found the tossed-veggie facial hydrating. And that special conditioning treatment did wonders for my hair."

Tristan laughed. "Kudos to you for being a good sport. Believe me, I know what a pain Asher can be." At this, Asher socked him in the arm. "But he's not so bad once you get to know him."

"I'm standing right here, you know," Asher snapped.

"Well, I don't see you doing any groveling, and you have to so you can go back to work," Tristan said. "Otherwise, you'll be grounded for the rest of your life and die of boredom." With that, he saluted Asher and headed down the hallway.

I swallowed down the lump of nerves stuck in my throat as I faced Asher alone. "So . . . Cleo asked me to talk to you about coming back," I said haltingly. "And it sounds like you don't have any other options anyway. . . ."

"I always have options," Asher quipped. "I don't need this job."

*Right*, I thought, *because you probably have a hefty trust fund that would pay for ten thousand vases.* But what I said was, "Well, anyway, we're shorthanded and Cleo needs someone. . . ."

"Yeah, someone who actually likes being crammed in a steel box for hours at a time."

"It's not a box, and you'd get used to it," I said, trying hard to keep my voice on an even keel as my anger flared again. Was it possible for him to say anything that was not completely offen-sive? "You might actually start to like it after a while. I do."

"Not a chance." He shook his head.

With that comment, my cheeks got hot as a griddle and my patience ran dry. "What is your problem, anyway?" I cried in exas-peration, throwing up my hands. "I'm trying to be nice, which, after yesterday, is no easy feat. Cleo thought I should give you the benefit of the doubt, though, so here I am. But this is just a colos-sal waste of time. Oh, and by the way, I'm pretty sure that even a penthouse can feel like a box when you're stuck in it forever. But let me know how being grounded for the rest of your life works out for you!" And with that, I whirled away from him and stomped down the hallway before he had a chance to say anything else.

When I sat down in the cafeteria for lunch, I was still fuming, and I couldn't wait to vent to Mei. I hadn't had a chance to fill her in on everything yet. Art history was our only class together this semester, and we'd spent the entire period debating over which artist to study for our big report. Mei wanted Coco Chanel because "fashion is art." I wanted Andy Warhol because, to him, food was art. To break the gridlock, Mr. Toulouse finally suggested an artist named Ansel Adams.

Now that we'd gotten that great debate out of the way, I was ready for a proper catch-up. But when Mei sat down across from me, she had Ben with her.

It wasn't like Ben had never sat with us before, but usually some of our other friends, like Leo and Ann, came along with him.

"Hey, Tessa," Mei and Ben said at the same time, then laughed at their in-sync-ness. I tried not to roll my eyes.

"So how's it going with Asher?" Mei asked as she and Ben sat down side by side. "You haven't told me yet."

"I know," I said, relieved and happy that in her state of Benfatuation she could still think properly. "You are not going to believe what happened. . . ."

Mei nodded, then held up a finger. "Yeah. I can't wait to hear. Just let Ben finish the story he was telling me in the cafeteria line. It was so funny."

Then, just like that, I lost her. She was tilting her head adoringly toward Ben, giggling away as he talked. By the time his story ended, so did lunch. I was walking quietly behind them on the way to our lockers when I caught Ben's fingers brush Mei's. This was not the least bit reassuring. They were probably only one day away from holding hands.

When we passed by the announcements bulletin board, Ben stopped.

"Hey." He pointed to a pink heart-shaped flyer. "You should sign up for that, Mei! It looks like fun."

I peeked over their shoulders to see that the heart flyer was a sign-up sheet for the Sweet Heart Ball decorating committee. Last year, since neither one of us had boys to go with, Mei and I hadn't gone to the Valentine's Day dance at all. Mei had been fine with that. From the dreamy smile on her face, though, I wasn't so sure about *this* year. Ben hadn't officially asked Mei to the dance. But since a guy never calls a dance "fun" unless he's planning on asking someone to go with him, it was probably only a matter of time.

I read the flyer again, and my stomach clenched. "The ball is *on* Valentine's Day this year," I said meekly. "That's the same day as the Great Pillow Fight."

"Oh," Mei said quietly, then added with fresh hope, "well, maybe we can do the pillow fight beforehand. The dance doesn't start until eight, and the pillow fight is at six."

"But when will we have time to get ready for the dance?" I asked. I knew getting ready quickly wouldn't be a problem for me, especially since I wasn't even sure I wanted to go to the dance at all. But Mei was another story. She took two hours just to get dressed to go to the mall. Getting dressed for a dance could take decades.

"We'll figure it out," Mei said cheerfully, and with Ben smiling encouragingly, she wrote her name next to *Committee Head*. Then the bell rang, and Ben offered to walk Mei to her class. They mumbled absentminded good-byes in my direction and then walked down the hallway.

I slumped against the wall. Now I understood why I've always felt sort of sorry for leftovers. At first, you find the food irresistible, but then you get tired of it. So the leftovers sit in the fridge watching you eat other things, waiting to get tossed out. And now I might be in serious danger of becoming a leftover, too.

# chapter
## four

On Thursday after school, I walked to the Tasty Truck in record time, partly because Mei wasn't with me, so there weren't any shopping pit stops. And partly because I was itching to get busy cooking to take my mind off Mei and Ben. The two of them had gone to get froyos after school, and as they were climbing onto the cable car together, I witnessed the first hand-holding moment.

As a best friend, I knew I was supposed to be happy for Mei, and I was trying to be. But lonely sometimes steps on happy's feet.

When I opened the back door of the truck, though, all my

hopes of spending the afternoon blissfully cooking in peace disappeared. Because there inside the truck, helping Gabe grill some chicken, was Asher.

"Tessa!" Gabe cried, lifting his tongs in greeting. "Look who decided to rejoin the team." He motioned enthusiastically at Asher, who was looking at me with a guarded, sullen expression. "Isn't that great?"

"Great," I echoed numbly.

"We're done grilling, so you can take over the training, T." Gabe handed me the tongs and slid the apron over his head. "Cleo went to the roof garden for more cilantro, but she'll be back later." He grabbed a stack of papers from the front of the truck. "I'm going to see if I can get some more signatures on these Flavorfest petitions."

"How many do you have so far?" I asked.

"Two," Gabe said. "Cleo's and mine."

"Make it three." I grabbed his pen and added my name to the petition. "Good luck," I added. As soon as Gabe was out the door, an uneasiness settled over the truck, and my heart sped up. Being near Asher, I felt a current of annoyance and adrenaline coursing through me, like I was both wanting and dreading another fight with him.

"I thought you weren't coming back," I said stiffly.

"I wasn't sure I was, either." He stared at the floor for a long time.

"What happened to all your other options?" I asked, knowing it was a zinger but not able to stop myself. "Did your mom freeze your savings account or something?"

He glared at me, and I could tell I'd probably hit pretty close to the mark.

"I already have enough to pay for the vase," he grumbled. "I just didn't *earn* it, so she won't let me use it."

"That's because she enjoys torturing you instead. Most parents do." I was surprised by the words as I said them. It almost felt like I was . . . confiding in Asher. How weird was that?

"That's so true," he said with a sigh. "The thing is, I shouldn't be here."

My teeth clenched. We were going down that road again? "Why?" I asked accusingly. "Because you're too good for it?"

"No! I know that's how it's coming across. But — but that's not it." He shook his head and was quiet for a long time, as if wrestling with what to say next. Finally, he spoke. "It's because . . . because I can't cook! At all! I set my microwave on fire making popcorn!"

I didn't mean to laugh, but I couldn't help myself. And after a moment, Asher joined in. When he smiled — not a Beautiful Person smile, poised for effect, but a real, genuine smile — he looked different, less guarded and even a little . . . sweet.

"I can top that," I said. "I once burned bread so badly the fire department had to come." I smiled back at him. "It just takes practice. I can show you the basics, but you have to try."

Asher thought about it for a minute, then reluctantly nodded. "I'll try."

I slid my apron over my head. "Okay, so we can start with sandwiches."

"Good," he said. "I love sandwiches."

"Making them, *not* eating them." I laughed. "Think of the Tasty Truck as a . . . baseball stadium," I said, trying to give him a way to relate to it. "Making sandwiches is sort of like swinging a baseball bat. The difference between a good 'wich and a bad 'wich is like the difference between a home run and a strike-out. A good 'wich is a crowd-pleaser — freshly made and *never* soggy. Serve a bad 'wich, and people leave the ballpark." I laid out all the ingredients for the Bacon Me Crazy BLT at the prep counter. "We'll start with the easiest and work our way up. Okay?"

He nodded. "Batter up."

An hour later, we had a dozen strikeouts and no home runs. It wasn't that Asher wasn't trying. He was, and for once, he wasn't being his obnoxious self. But he put too much sauce on Nick's BLT, and when Nick bit into it, the sauce oozed out all over his basketball uniform. Asher put beef instead of turkey on some-one's Gobble Me Up, and doubled the feta when a customer asked for *no* cheese on her Chic Greek. *And* she was vegan, so that didn't go over so well. By the time I gave her a refund, Asher and I were both exhausted and out of patience.

"This is crazy," he grumbled. "Making a sandwich shouldn't be this hard. I mean, it's *just* a sandwich."

"*Just* a sandwich?" My voice rose a few notches. "These are not slapdash PB&Js. They're not prepackaged, preservative-filled insta-wraps. Do you have any idea what really goes into making one of these?"

"Obviously not." He glared at me. "Because if I did, people wouldn't be asking for their money back!" He kicked at one of the cabinets, then stormed out of the truck. I hesitated, then followed him.

Even though it was only four o'clock, the winter sun was already low in the sky, and the buildings were shaded with dusk. A salty breeze whisked up sharp from the bay, cooling my temper some, but not completely.

"This is a mistake!" he said, pacing the sidewalk. "I'm never going to get the hang of it."

"Well, you won't if you keep quitting!" I cried. "I've never seen anyone give up so easily! Haven't you ever had to work for anything in your life?"

His frown deepened with embarrassment. "Up until now, no," he muttered.

Of course not. I took a deep breath to try to calm down, then made a spur-of-the-moment decision.

"Wait here," I said to Asher, then quickly texted Cleo. When I heard back from her, I went back inside the truck and locked it up tight.

"What are you doing?" he asked sullenly.

"Closing early," I said. "Cleo said it was okay. She'll come back to finish up the rest." I faced him squarely. "So . . . you think our truck sells 'just' sandwiches. Nothing special, right?" I turned in the direction of home, then waved for him to follow. "Come with me. There's something I want you to see."

When I opened the door to the roof of our townhouse, the rosy sky had deepened to indigo. The lights from the townhouses were blinking on, one by one, and the Golden Gate Bridge was throwing a twinkling reflection onto the bay. Off to the right, the skyscrapers of the financial district blazed in a golden glow, with the Transamerica Pyramid seeming to pierce the dark sky with its needlelike tip.

I flipped a switch in the stairwell beside the door, and the hundreds of bulbs strung across the edges of our rooftop flickered on, bathing it in soft white light.

"This is where our sandwiches start," I said to Asher.

He looked around, and I tried to take it all in through *his* eyes: the raised beds of soil full of fresh rosemary, oregano, and cilantro; the climbing tomato plants; the small crops of cucumbers, peppers, arugula, and potatoes that sprouted up from the soil we'd spread underneath miniature plastic greenhouse covers so they'd be protected from the chilly San Fran winter nights.

"All of our ingredients come from this garden," I said, making sure to speak softly, which is what I always did when I was up on the roof, not wanting to disturb all the growing going on. I loved it up here almost as much as I loved cooking in the kitchen. "Everything we use is homegrown and organic, except for our meat, of course. But even that's hormone- and antibiotic-free."

"Wow," Asher said, the grudging look on his face softening. He bent down to brush his hand across one of the tomato plants. "That's pretty cool."

"I know," I said, my frustration easing just a bit. "I get defensive about it because not too many people understand. We're not your average fast-food joint."

"I guess I've been sounding pretty jerky about the whole thing, huh?" he admitted quietly.

"Um . . . slightly," I said with a laugh.

He tucked his hands into his pockets. "Well, you get so bossy when you're trying to show me things in the truck."

I stiffened. "Maybe I wouldn't be so pushy if you didn't act so stuck-up all the time."

We glared at each other, then both started laughing.

"What if we both try to cut each other some slack?" I finally said. "Then maybe we won't actually kill each other?"

"That's a big maybe," he said, "but I'm willing if you are."

I nodded, then picked up my hand shovel and spread some fresh compost and dirt around the bottom of one of the tomato plants. "So, are you going to help me, or are you afraid your hands will get too dirty?" I said in a tentative teasing tone to see how he'd react.

He snorted, then dropped to his knees smiling. "If that's your idea of cutting me some slack, we're in trouble."

"Sorry." I laughed and handed him a shovel. "Couldn't resist."

We worked side by side for a few minutes, and then Asher sat back on his heels. "You know, I don't even know what half these plants are. That's part of my problem. How can I cook when I don't have any idea what I'm cooking with?"

"Well, here." I pushed a stray curl off my forehead, bent down, and pinched a sprig from an oregano plant, then held it up under his nose. "Tell me what it smells like."

He took a deep breath. "Like . . . baked ziti takeout from Dimitri's."

I laughed. "That's right. It's oregano, but you don't need to know what its name is; you just need to know what works together. Blending is what makes recipes great."

I pulled a few more herbs, and he nailed the dishes they were used in every time. "You can do it," I said finally, "you just need to be patient."

"Wait a sec." He smirked and shot me a look. "*I'm* the one who needs to be patient?"

He held my gaze until I giggled. "Okay, we *both* need more patience."

He nodded. "I can live with that." He sat down on the brick patio and leaned back on his elbows, and I sat down next to him. "It's so peaceful up here," he said. "I bet without the city lights you could see Cassiopeia."

"You know about Cassiopeia?" I repeated in disbelief. When I was little, Dad read me the myths more often than fairy tales. It was important for me to know the foundations of my Greekness, he said, the roots of my ancestors. I knew my myths, but I didn't think too many other kids at Bayview did.

But Asher nodded. "Sure. It's a constellation, named after a queen in Greek mythology. She was so vain she boasted that she was more beautiful than the sea god's own daughters. So as punishment, Poseidon banished her to the stars." He looked up. "At this time of night, Cassiopeia would be right about . . . there." He pointed into the sky, but the rooftop lights made it impossible to see anything.

As he talked, a bright excitement came into his face, nothing like the detached vibe he'd been giving off. My expression must have been one of surprise, because he laughed. "What? So . . . I know a little bit about stars."

"A little?" I said doubtfully.

"Okay . . . a lot," he said. "I'm a secret member of the San Fran Kids' Astronomy Club."

"Why secret?" I asked.

"I just never got around to telling anybody else, I guess."

I studied his face and saw a hint of discomfort in it. "Never got around to it, or didn't *want* to tell anybody else?"

"I don't know," he said. "Stargazing isn't exactly the coolest extracurricular activity, you know?"

"If it's what you like to do, who cares about what's cool?"

He dropped his eyes, and that was the second I knew how much *he* cared, or at least how much he cared about his friends caring. It explained a lot about the way he acted in general.

"Can I tell you something?" he asked after we'd sat in silence for a minute. "I broke my mom's vase on purpose."

I stared at him. "Why?"

He dug his shoe into a crevice in the patio. "It was the last thing my dad gave her before he left. They got divorced about a year ago. I didn't think she'd miss it. I just . . . didn't want it in our house anymore."

"Oh. Sorry," I said awkwardly, surprised by his sudden honesty. For a second, he'd dropped his defenses, and I caught a fleeting glimpse of what he might be like behind the Great Wall of Snobbishness.

"So maybe we should work on a sandwich named after a star," I said, changing the subject. "Cassiopeia could be a great name for a new sandwich, and it could be your first original recipe."

Asher thought about it. "What about . . . the Cassio*pita*?"

"Brilliant!" I cried. "I love it already."

"Really?" a sharp voice snipped behind me.

There was Karrie, framed in the doorway of the stairwell with her lips pursed and one hand pressed against her hip. She gave Asher a piercing look, and Asher's Great Wall instantly rose again. "Did you forget that you were supposed to meet Tristan and me at the marina?" Karrie demanded. "We were waiting forever, so finally I went to *that* truck and the woman sent me here."

"Sorry," Asher said, standing up. "I lost track of time." He glanced at me. "I should get going."

"Okay," I said. "See you later."

He waved and they turned toward the stairs, but then Karrie

looked back, a patronizing smile playing at the corners of her mouth.

"Um, you know you have dirt on your face, right?" she said.

"Sure," I said, not missing a beat. "You've heard of mud masks. You should give it a try sometime."

Asher coughed a laugh into his sleeve while Karrie's eyes flashed fire. She disappeared down the stairs without another word, but Asher hesitated for a second longer. There seemed to be an unspoken apology in his eyes.

"Thanks for tonight," he said. "It was fun."

I laughed at the note of surprise in his voice. "Hey, I can be fun, you know."

"When you're not in Tasty-Truck-command-mode," he said. "See you later."

His genuine smile as he left sent an unexpected flutter of excitement through me. What had just happened? It was like there were two versions of Asher now: the rich-boy brat with a chip on his shoulder; and the deeper, more authentic guy. I wasn't sure which version was real, but now that we'd finally broken the ice, maybe I'd be able to find out.

The phone was ringing when I got downstairs, and when I picked it up, Mei was on the other end of the line.

"Hey," she said. "Do you have plans on Saturday?"

"Cleo and I are taking the Tasty Truck to the Bayview baseball game on Saturday afternoon, but I don't have anything before that. Why?"

"I thought we could go to the de Young Museum to get started on our Ansel Adams project. They have a special exhibit of his photography going on right now. It could have some good info."

"Definitely." I nodded. "I'll double-check with Mom and Dad, but let's plan on it." It would be so nice to have some one-on-one time with Mei.

"Great," she said. "Hey, I want the Asher update, too. I know Ben and I sort of hogged the talk-time at lunch."

"Oh!" I smiled into the phone, thrilled that for the moment, Mei sounded like her everyday, pre-Ben self. "Well, Tuesday was a complete disaster, but then today —"

There was a click, and then Mei said, "Oh, Tessa, it's Ben on the other line. Do you mind if I grab it? I'll call you right back afterward, okay?"

My heart sank. "Sure," I said. "No problem." But she'd already hung up.

Over the next hour, I finished all my homework, had dinner with Mom and Dad, packed my lunch for the next day, and looked at a dozen Ansel Adams photos online. But Mei didn't call.

I thought about calling her back, but I didn't, because I wanted her to remember. I wanted her to *want* to call back.

When she didn't, I decided I needed to focus on something else, and that something else was cooking.

I knocked on the door of Mom and Dad's shared home office. Mom was there, her eyes focused on her double computer screens, the ones that can show her the US and Asian stock markets at the same time.

"Mom, is it okay if I go upstairs to Cleo's for a while?" I asked. "I did all my homework, and I thought I'd work on a couple recipes."

Mom looked at me from over her screens. "I was actually just about to log off for tonight. Do you want to go get some ice cream at the marina?"

"Not really," I said, thinking that if we ran into Asher and his friends, I'd have to put up with more searing looks from Karrie. But then disappointment flickered across Mom's face, and I felt a stab of guilt. "Sorry, Mom, I've just had a bummer night so far. All I want to do is get my hands on some veggies and a cutting board."

"Oh," Mom said, nodding. "Stress relief. I get it." I knew she was trying to draw a connection, but she looked like she was drawing a complete blank. "Well, do you want to talk about what's bugging you?"

"Not so much." I shook my head.

Mom looked at me for a long minute. Then her eyes flicked back to her computer screens, and I could tell she was diving back into her numbers. "Okay, then, have fun with Cleo," she said. "Just be back down by bedtime."

I nodded, and then climbed the stairs to Cleo's pad. She and Gabe were busy baking fresh bread for tomorrow's sandwiches, singing at the top of their lungs to the Beatles' "Across the Universe."

Cleo threw me a ball of dough and waved me over to the counter.

"How did the petitions go?" I asked Gabe.

"Fifty signatures and counting," he said proudly. "All of the food-truck owners are up in arms over getting booted from the Taste of San Fran festival."

"That's great!" I high-fived him.

"Great, yes," Cleo said. "Enough? No. But we'll keep on trying. A bunch of us are going in front of the city council next Monday night. We'll see if we can make some progress then, but Mr. Morgan isn't happy about the meeting. I was renewing one of the truck's permits at the Department of Health and Sanitation today and saw him there. He was talking to a clerk about recent complaints filed on food trucks. So I'm sure he'll show up on Monday fully armed with stories that make food trucks look bad."

"I don't get it," I said. "Why does he have to try to make food trucks look bad to make his restaurants look good?"

Cleo shrugged. "If food trucks have a bad rap, then nobody will think he's a jerk for canceling Flavorfest. It's a dirty game he's playing, but we can't let him mess with our heads when we have a business to run. So" — she gave me a playful hip bump — "get cooking."

I grinned. "You don't have to ask me twice." Within minutes, I was belting out the Beatles right along with them. After we'd finished making the bread and I'd diced and sliced veggies to my heart's content, I went back downstairs for bed.

When I passed Mom's office, she'd fallen asleep in her chair. I bent to wake her, and I saw that, instead of her stock-market numbers, the screen glowed with a different Internet page: cookingfordummies.com.

I studied Mom's face, more relaxed in sleep than I ever saw it when she was in work-mode. Was she trying to learn to cook? Why, when she'd always said she hated cooking?

Mei, Asher, Mom — everyone around me was changing. And I wasn't sure how I felt about any of it.

# chapter
# five

I checked my watch for the third time. 9:15 A.M.

Mom had dropped me off at the main entrance to the de Young Museum, but she was waiting in the parking lot until I went inside. Right now, she was probably sitting in the car wondering the same thing I was. *Where is Mei?*

My best friend was supposed to have met me there at nine o'clock, and she was never late. I was just dialing Mei's cell when I glanced up to see her walking toward me, arm in arm with Ben. I sagged inwardly.

The de Young Museum is part of the sprawling grounds of

Golden Gate Park. I'd thought that after the museum, Mei and I could grab some ice cream and hang out in the park. But none of that seemed as much fun with Ben in tow.

Still, though, I wanted to be a good sport about it. So I tried to smile cheerfully at both of them.

"Sorry we're late," Mei said. "Mom made us take the twins to the carousel and then we walked from there."

Ben nodded. "Mei took me through the Shakespeare Garden on the way. She recited about twenty lines from *Love's Labour's Lost* by heart! I couldn't believe it."

"It wasn't a big deal." Mei blushed. Then she glanced at me with mild surprise, like she'd just remembered I was there. "Were you waiting long?"

"Not really," I said breezily, struggling not to show my annoyance. "But we should probably go inside and get started."

"Sure," Mei said.

Once we walked inside and headed in the direction of the Ansel Adams exhibit, though, Mei threw me for another loop.

"Ben's doing his report on Mary Cassatt and that's in a different hall," she said, checking out her museum map. Then she looked at me. "Maybe you could get started with the Ansel Adams, and we'll meet you there in a little while?"

My insides twisted uncomfortably. So she was going to help Ben with his art project while I worked on *ours*?

"But, we're supposed to work on it together," I argued.

"We will," Mei said. "I'll only be about fifteen minutes, okay?"

"Okay," my mouth said while my mind hollered, *No way!*

As they walked away, I sighed, then took out my notebook and pen. This day was rapidly going from disappointing to dismal.

Mei's fifteen minutes soon turned into forty-five. I walked around the exhibit hall again . . . and again. At first, it felt peaceful to wander through the expansive white rooms with their soft lighting and shiny wooden floors. Ansel Adams's black-and-white photographs of the waterfalls and mountains of Yosemite National Park were beautiful. And his photographs of San Francisco took my breath away.

I read about how he had worked to protect the environment, not just in national parks but in San Francisco, too. When he learned that there were plans to build high-rise apartments in the hills surrounding the Golden Gate Bridge, Ansel pasted pictures of apartment buildings onto one of his Golden Gate photos and then hung the photo in a storefront. His protest helped prevent the apartments from being built. As I read that, I couldn't help wondering if Ansel would've thought that Flavorfest was something about San Francisco that was worth saving, too.

A tap on my shoulder interrupted my thoughts, and I turned to see Mei and Ben.

"Are you ready to get started?" Mei asked.

She *had* to be kidding. I knew so much about Ansel Adams by this point I probably could've given the report right then and there. "I already went through the exhibit three times," I snapped. "I took a ton of notes."

"Great!" Mei said, oblivious to my irritation. "I'll just take a quick look around."

My cell phone vibrated. "That's my mom," I said. Mei and Ben had disappeared for so long, I'd called Mom. My mood was shot, and so were any hopes I'd had of hanging out with Mei alone. All I wanted to do was leave. "She's outside to pick me up."

"Oh." Mei's face fell. "Do you have to leave already? Ben and I were going to check out the arboretum."

"They have a corpse flower on exhibit," Ben said. "I heard it smells so bad some people faint when they get near it. Cool, huh?"

"Wow, Mei, I can't believe you want to smell it," I said. "You couldn't even handle the worm dissection in Mrs. Cheever's class, remember? She had to send you to the nurse's office."

"Oh, that was because I was coming down with the flu," Mei said, laughing and waving her hand dismissively. "I'll be fine."

Her voice had taken on a high-pitched cheeriness, and I stared at her. Either Mei had suddenly learned to love grossness, or her enthusiasm was all for Ben's benefit.

"Sorry I have to miss it," I said, to be polite, though after how the morning had gone, I wasn't sorry at all. "I have to meet Cleo at the Tasty Truck for the baseball game, though. I'll e-mail you my notes, Mei."

"Okay," Mei said. "Have fun at the game. I'll call you later."

I knew she probably wouldn't. When I got into Mom's car, I leaned my head against the window, imagining Mei fainting at the smell of the corpse flower and Ben catching her swiftly in his arms. That would be perfect for Mei, just like some romantic scene in one of her plays. Up until now, I'd always had a front-row seat in our friendship, watching and cheering her on. But for the first time ever, I found myself wondering whether she noticed. Maybe Mei didn't care if I was in the audience at all.

When Cleo parked the Tasty Truck next to the bleachers at the Bayview baseball field, I breathed a sigh of relief. I needed a distraction to take my mind off Mei and Ben. The day was cool but sunny — perfect weather for baseball — and the bleachers were packed. Within minutes of us firing up the grill, we had our first few customers.

"Sports work up an appetite," Cleo said to me after we'd made our tenth BLT. "Even if you're just watching."

I laughed, but in between customers, I'd been watching the game, too. Actually, I'd mostly been watching Asher.

I'd never paid much attention to his jock status at school, because my world revolves around sandwiches, not sports. But on the field, Asher was something to see. His pitch was smooth and lightning fast, and it made me smile to see the rival coach's face get progressively redder with each player Asher struck out. By the top of the ninth, it was obvious that Bayview was going to win, mostly because of the game Asher had pitched.

And by then, I had to admit that Asher looked pretty adorable in his baseball uniform.

The second the game was over, there was a mad rush to the Tasty Truck. I was so busy making sandwiches as Cleo called out the orders that I didn't even notice Asher and Tristan in the line.

"Can you make mine with double bacon and extra sauce?" Asher asked with a grin, startling me.

My breath quickened, but I recovered in time. "Anything for the star player," I said teasingly.

Tristan frowned dramatically. "And what about me? Don't I get any credit for that home run I hit at the top of the seventh?"

I rolled my eyes. "Oh, excuse me. I meant star *players*, plural."

Tristan bowed. "Thank you."

"Hey!" a man suddenly yelled from the back of the very long line. "Can you hurry it up? It's a famine back here."

"Oops, I better get back to it before they eat the truck," I told Tristan and Asher. Then I glanced at Cleo, who was piling bacon on the grill with one hand and trying to wrap a finished sandwich with the other. I could see we were starting to get behind with our orders. "Hey, Asher," I called to him as he walked toward Karrie and his other waiting friends, "do you think you could help out for a little bit? We're seriously swamped."

"Um . . ." Asher glanced at Tristan, Karrie, and the other Beautiful People.

"Go for it," a boy named Cole snickered. "I'm *dying* to see you flipping some bacon."

Karrie glanced at Asher, an unspoken challenge in her eyes. Then, in a voice loud enough for everyone in the line to hear, she said, "Asher would never be caught dead working in that grease pit on his day off."

All the kids in Asher's group laughed, except Tristan and Asher. Asher glanced down. It was only a millisecond, but I saw it on his face — a flash of shame.

"Actually," Asher mumbled to me, "I should go. We're heading to get frozen yogurt and everyone's waiting. . . ."

I nodded, my cheeks flaming. Just when I had started to hope Asher was a better guy than I'd first thought, he had to pull something like this. And why? To show off for Karrie?

"Right." I swallowed down my disappointment. "Have fun."

I glanced at Karrie's triumphant smirk. And then, before I knew what I was doing, I leaned out of the window of the truck. "Karrie, I meant to tell you earlier how much I love the color of your lip gloss." I smiled sweetly. "Did you know that there's lard in a lot of lip glosses? There are just *so* many great uses for pork grease, don't you think?"

Karrie's face morphed from shock to rage, and she stomped away through the crowd. My momentary glee was replaced with panic. Omigod. Had I just tried to put the Bayview Queen Bee in her place? It was like signing a social death warrant. Asher looked back at me once, but then he was gone with the rest. Tristan was the only one who hesitated, grinning at me.

"What you said to Karrie just then?" He gave me a thumbs-up. "Awesome. No one ever stands up to her."

"Thanks," I mumbled. "Especially not Asher, huh?"

Tristan shrugged. "Asher's parents used to fight a lot before their divorce, so I guess he doesn't like to stir things up."

I felt a pang of sudden understanding, remembering how Asher had opened up to me on the roof.

"Gotta go," Tristan said, backing up a few paces. "I'll be back at the truck after school on Monday for another BLT. You can count on it."

"Somebody sure likes BLTs," Cleo said, watching Tristan as he walked away. "Or maybe there's another reason he wants to come back for more?" She gave me a sly grin.

"What?" I said, drawing a blank. But then I caught her meaning and blushed. "N-no," I stammered. Then, more adamantly, "No! Tristan? There's no way that . . ."

"That what? He might like you?" Cleo said. "And why wouldn't he? You're quite likeable, Tessa, whether you realize it or not."

I let Cleo's words sink in. I'd never thought of myself as someone a boy — let alone a Beautiful People boy like Tristan — might have a crush on.

It was true that Tristan was always friendly toward me, and that he was showing up at the truck more and more often. And I probably should've felt flattered, but instead, the thought made my stomach churn uneasily.

On Sunday morning, I woke up to an empty house; Mom and Dad both had to work that day. So I tucked myself cozily into the kitchen to play with food. That's how I always thought of my recipes, as playing, because it was so much fun to scan the contents of the fridge, garden, and pantry for intriguing ingredients.

Today, I had a plan to try out two new creations: bacon jam and peanut-butter-bacon cookies. Luckily, I found the most crucial ingredient in the fridge: lots and lots of bacon.

Once the bacon was sizzling in the skillet, the kitchen filled with a warm, crisp, smoky scent. It was a scent that said all was right with the world, and it made you want to believe it, even when you knew it couldn't possibly be true.

I breathed in deep, then grabbed a piece of crisp, still-crackling bacon and popped it in my mouth. Mmmm. Even if we just sold strips of bacon straight off the griddle at the truck, and nothing else, we could probably keep our customers happy. Bacon was just that darn good.

After I'd chopped the bacon into tiny bits, I sautéed some onions and garlic, then tossed half the bacon in with it. Then, I added brown sugar, a hefty dollop of maple syrup, a splash of balsamic vinegar, and finally, a spoonful of mustard. While the mix was simmering, I started on the batch of peanut-butter cookies, loving the feel of the sticky batter as I rolled it between my fingers.

The messier my hands got, the calmer I felt. Slowly but surely, my frustrations about Mei and Ben, about Asher and Tristan and Karrie and Flavorfest, began to work their way out through my fingertips.

Soon, the first batches of cookies and jam were ready. The jam was a beautiful cranberry color and smelled amazing, and I thought I had a winner. But then I tasted it. In theory, I believed that bacon could make pretty much anything taste better. But in jam? Not so much. I couldn't even swallow the bite I took. Cleo told me the best chefs always admit to their mistakes, and the bacon jam was an utterly gag-worthy one. So I threw the jam away with a sigh.

The peanut-butter cookies, on the other hand, were divine. Cooking is a little like baseball, I guess: You win some, you lose some.

"I hope you didn't pack a lunch," I said to Mei when I sat down in art history on Monday morning, "because I thought you could do some taste-testing for me? I went on a little bit of a cooking spree yesterday."

She caught sight of the cooler I was holding, and her jaw dropped. "Omigod," she said. "The last time you did that was right after you forgot to study for your history test and you failed it." She leaned toward me. "What's wrong?"

"Everything." I was so relieved she was honing in on my mood for the first time in days that I wanted to hug her. "Asher's still copping an attitude about the Tasty Truck, I may have started a war with Karrie, Flavorfest is probably going to get canceled, and . . ." *And you're so busy being Ben's girlfriend that you forgot about me.* It was right there on the tip of my tongue, but I stopped it before it poured out.

Then Mr. Toulouse walked in, and Mei silently mouthed, "Talk more at lunch?"

I nodded, my heart skipping happily. Maybe Mei was back to her old self.

But when noon came, Mei flagged me down in the hallway outside the cafeteria.

"Tessa," she said. "I forgot that I have my first decoration meeting for the Sweet Heart Ball during lunch today. But I told Ben and Leo about the food you brought, and they're dying to try everything. They rallied a bunch of their friends to be your taste-testers, too."

"Great," I said, trying to disguise my disappointment. "In other words, I get to spend my lunch hour watching a bunch of boys inhale my works of art and then burp out critiques?"

"Something like that." Mei laughed and shrugged. "But I'm sure Ben will give you some good feedback. And I'll call you later and we'll make plans to do something fun this weekend, okay?"

"Okay," I said, mustering up a good-natured smile.

Then I squared my shoulders and walked into the cafeteria with my cooler. I saw Asher at the Beautiful People table, watching as I laid out the food. But when I glanced his way, he turned back to his friends, avoiding my eyes. Good. Let him feel guilty about what he'd done on Saturday. He should. I noticed Tristan at the table, too, and when he waved to me, I looked quickly away. Why were boys so confusing?

Ben and the cavemen showed up then, and there was nothing confusing about them: They were hungry, and they wanted to try my bacony treats. They finished off the bacon-bits brownies and maple-bacon cupcakes in under two minutes, and afterward, the only feedback I got was a monosyllabic "Good." Sigh. So much for my discerning taste-testers.

# chapter
# six

At the Tasty Truck that afternoon, things felt frosty between me and Asher. And when Cleo went to the rooftop garden for more tomatoes and Gabe left for his class, I couldn't help but say something.

"So," I said coolly as I placed a slice of bread in the toaster, "did you enjoy your frozen yogurt after the game?"

Asher shook his head. "I knew you wouldn't let it go," he said, frowning. His knife came down faster on the onions he was chopping, and I noticed that he was getting better at cutting, even in one week's time. "I saw that look you gave me on Saturday," he said. "You think I'm a complete sellout."

"I didn't say that." My face warmed under his gaze. Ugh. How could he make me this flustered even when I was mad at him? "I just want to know why it's so embarrassing for you to be seen working in this truck."

"I don't think it's embarrassing," he said quietly and firmly. He sighed. "Look. My friends think of me a certain way, and it's easier for me if that doesn't change."

"I don't get it," I sputtered. "Why would you hang out with people who want you to act like someone you're not? They don't sound like any kind of friends I've ever had."

"That's because you wouldn't put up with my kind of friends," Asher said matter-of-factly. "I saw that about you when I first met you. You have other things that are important to you besides your rank at school, like this truck. You love it. But some of us don't have things like that."

"You have your baseball, and your astronomy . . ." I started.

He waved his hand. "None of my friends even know about

the astronomy thing," he said quietly. "That's what I mean. Everybody has their own comfort zone. You have yours, and I have mine."

"But it doesn't have to be that way," I persisted.

He looked at me doubtfully. "Really? So, say Tristan and I plunked ourselves down at the table today in the cafeteria for your taste-test — it would've been fine?"

"Sure," I said, and inside I wondered: *Had Asher* wanted *to join the taste test?* "I mean, maybe some kids would've whispered. . . ." I rethought. "Or maybe all of them would've. But who cares?"

He stared at the counter for a long minute. "Maybe it's not as easy for me as it is for you," he finally said. We were quiet for a moment. "You don't have to like my social scene," Asher added, stepping closer to level his eyes with mine. "But you can't keep judging me all the time for it, or *we'll* never be the kind of friends who talk about real stuff. And I was sort of hoping we could be."

His amber eyes were intense. Heat flashed over my face, and suddenly I found it hard to breathe. The rest of the lecture that I had mapped out in my mind flitted away, and all I could say was a quiet "Okay."

He needed a true friend, and he was giving me the chance to be one. If I believed everything I'd just spouted off about not caring about social rules, then I had to say yes. But more important, I *wanted* to say yes.

He smiled at me. "Okay."

"Hey!" A voice made us both jump, and within seconds, we were each at separate ends of the truck, and Tristan's head was leaning in the window, grinning mischievously at us. "What are you two looking so guilty about? Don't tell me you're out of bacon?"

"One BLT, coming right up," I said, turning away to hide my burning cheeks. I busied myself stacking the sandwich. "I have a new dessert today, too," I added. "Bacon-peanut-butter cookies."

Tristan smacked his lips. "Must . . . feed . . . bacon . . . cravin' . . . now."

I laughed as I handed him two cookies. He took a big bite out of the first one. "Mmmm . . . tell Cleo I'm in love," he said.

"I'm flattered, bud, but I'm spoken for," Cleo said, climbing into the truck. "And besides," she added, winking at me, "Tessa made them. She came up with the recipe yesterday."

Tristan tipped an imaginary hat in my direction. "You just get cooler by the minute," he said. "Any chance your parents would consider adopting me?"

I scoffed. "Not the way you eat. Our pantries would be bare in twenty-four hours."

"It was worth a try." He shrugged, then said something to Asher about meeting up later, and left.

"He's becoming quite the regular," Cleo said after he was gone. "But he only stops by when you're here, Tessa." She gave me a knowing grin. "I'm pretty sure I just witnessed some flirting going on?"

I could feel Asher's eyes on my face, and embarrassment coursed through me.

"Not at all," I said vehemently.

"Tristan's not flirting," Asher said, his voice suddenly sounding flat and slightly impatient. "He jokes like that with everyone."

I was grateful he was giving me an out, but I felt a small sting at his words, too. Why was he dismissing the possibility so quickly? Was it that hard to believe Tristan would flirt with me?

"Look, can we just drop it already?" I cried. "There's no flirting, there's no crushing. There's nothing, okay?"

Cleo held up her hands. "Sorry," she said softly. "I was just kidding around."

I sighed, "No, it's okay. Let's just . . . forget it."

As we got ready to close up shop early so that Cleo could get to her city council meeting, I tried to pin down why I was getting so riled up. But when Asher accidentally brushed against me and I felt a wave of breathlessness, I knew the answer. I didn't want Cleo teasing me about Tristan in front of Asher, because I didn't want Asher thinking Tristan liked me, or that I liked Tristan. It was completely irrational, but so was the dizzying giddiness I was starting to feel around Asher more and more.

At five o'clock, my heart instinctively sped up, because I knew at that moment, Cleo was going before the city council with her petitions to save Flavorfest.

I was in the kitchen making *yigandes plaki*. It was one of Cleo's favorite Greek casseroles, and I was making it to surprise her when she came home. But so far, I'd checked the clock so many times I'd only managed to dice one single tomato. At the rate I was going, dinner would be ready sometime next year.

I didn't even notice when Mom came out of her office until she touched my shoulder, making me jump.

"Everything okay?" she asked. "You didn't even hear me calling your name."

I nodded. "I'm fine. Just wondering how the meeting's going for Cleo."

Mom smiled. "I'm sure Cleo's giving them an earful about the importance of supporting food-truck businesses and community bonding."

"Yeah, and I bet the only bonding Mr. Morgan does is with his champagne and caviar," I quipped.

Mom's lips tightened. "Don't be so quick to judge, Tessa. He's trying to do what's best for his restaurants. They're probably as important to him as the Tasty Truck and Flavorfest are to Cleo."

"Well, why can't he put his five-star entrées on display right alongside our sandwiches?"

"Because sandwiches aren't the same as fine dining, Tessa," Mom said.

I bristled. Why wasn't talking to Mom ever simple?

Mom sighed, then stretched. "You know, I've been staring at my computer screen all day. I could use a break." She glanced down at the tomatoes. "Do you need some help cooking?"

I froze. Never once had Mom offered to help me in the kitchen. When Cleo taught me how to cook and Mom and Dad deemed me "oven-safe," they were both more than happy to turn the kitchen over to me. In fact, Mom was always saying that if it weren't for me and Cleo, we'd be subsisting on takeout. But now here she was, wanting to help. Bizarre.

"Um, sure," I said, handing her a bowl of minced garlic and onions. "You can sauté these for me."

"Okay!" Mom said enthusiastically. She dumped everything into a skillet and turned on the burner.

"Don't forget the EVOO," I said.

"The what?" Mom asked blankly.

"Extra-virgin olive oil." I handed her the bottle.

"Got it," Mom said, pouring some in. "What next?"

"When the onions get transparent and a little caramel-colored, they're ready," I said, smiling at her. I had to admit, it was nice to have Mom in the kitchen working with me, and it made me feel like I wanted to share more with her. I put the tomato sauce on to simmer, then said, "Can you keep an eye on this for a sec? I want to grab something out of my room. I made these peanut-butter cookies yesterday. You have to try one. . . ."

She nodded, so I went to my room to get the last few cookies from the cooler. I was only gone a minute or two, but when I came back into the kitchen, Mom was MIA, and the onions had charred to black in the skillet.

I turned off the burner, frowning. Then I peeked into Mom's office and saw her on her cell phone, talking about stocks in her business voice.

When she came back into the kitchen, she eyed the pile of burnt onions in the sink. "I'm sorry, honey," she said. "I had to take that phone call, and I just stepped away for a second. . . ."

"It's okay, Mom," I said, hearing the disappointment in my voice.

Mom checked her watch. "I've got to make one more phone call." She already had one foot in her office when she called back. "Oh, wasn't there something you wanted to show me?"

I sighed. What was the point? She'd eat one of the cookies and make some polite remark about them being tasty, but she wouldn't really get it. I wasn't sure she ever would. "Never mind," I called back, swallowing down the lump in my throat. "It's no big deal."

Mom and I were just sitting down to the casserole when Dad walked in the front door.

"Guess who I found sitting on our front steps drowning her sorrows in a bacon-bits brownie?" he asked, and Cleo walked in behind him.

"How'd the meeting go?" Mom asked.

From the crestfallen look on Cleo's face, I knew the answer before she said a word.

"No Flavorfest this year," she said. "Mr. Morgan offered to pay triple the price for the space where Flavorfest is normally held. So, he'll hold the Taste of San Fran, without the food trucks. We've been ousted."

"But — but what about the petitions?" I stammered. "You had hundreds of signatures. . . ."

Cleo smiled at me sadly, sinking down into a chair. "It's not enough. Mr. Morgan has a lot of pull in this town, and the council listens to his wallet. The council members said they sympathized with the plight of the food trucks, but there's nothing they can do. None of the parks in the city are zoned properly for a fair like Flavorfest, and the other places that might've worked are booked already." She sighed. "I'm just worried that if we don't have Flavorfest this year, we'll never have it again."

"It's so disappointing," Dad said.

Cleo nodded. "It would've been a huge boost for our business. If the Bacon Me Crazy BLT had won the Flavorfest Best Award, Gabe and I could've counted on keeping the truck running through next year guaranteed."

My stomach plunged. "What do you mean? Are you going to close the truck?"

"I hope not," Cleo said. "But food trucks don't usually survive forever." She sighed. "I didn't want to tell you before, but . . . we've been struggling. Everyone loves our sandwiches, but we're just not as successful as the other trucks. I was hoping that winning the Flavorfest award would guarantee a longer life for the Tasty Truck, but without the award, I don't know what will happen."

We sat in silence for a few minutes, then I stood up to fix Cleo and Dad dinner plates. "I made *yigandes plaki*, your favorite," I said weakly to Cleo.

But Cleo got to her feet, looking a little pale. "Thanks, but I'm going to pass. My stomach's in knots." She gave us a small smile. "One too many bacon-bits brownies on the walk home." She turned toward the stairs. "See you all in the A.M."

I felt as depressed as Cleo looked. "I'm not hungry anymore, either," I told my parents. "Is it okay if I go start my homework?"

Mom nodded, but once I got to my room, I didn't even open my backpack. Instead, I dialed Mei's number, because right now, more than anything, I needed to talk to her.

"Guess what?" she shrieked into the phone before I even had a chance to say hi. "Ben just invited me to go with him to the Teen Music Fest at the Rickshaw Stop this Saturday night!"

"That's great," I said halfheartedly. "I'm sure it'll be awesome."

"It will be," she said "But my parents won't let me go unless you come, too. They're worried about me being alone with Ben in a dark theater." She giggled, then whispered, "Too many places for kissing, I guess."

"Wait a sec," I said. "*Have* you kissed Ben?"

"Not yet," she whispered. "But I think I want to. . . ."

"Wow," I said. "That's huge." I'd never been kissed. Or even come close to it.

"So . . . will you come? Please?"

I wasn't in a concert kind of mood. But I didn't want to let Mei down, either. Especially now that things seemed to be getting back to normal between us.

"I'll check with my parents," I said, then had to hold the phone away from my ear while she screamed into it.

"Thankyouthankyouthankyouthankyou!" she yelled. "Oh, it's going to be so much fun. Omigod, I have to figure out what I'm going to wear, and then I have to figure out what *you're* going to wear."

"*That's* not happening," I said, smiling in spite of myself. "But I will consult you if the need arises."

Mei clucked her tongue. "Party pooper." I could hear shuffling on the other end of the line, and I guessed she was flipping through clothes in her closet. "Ugh, I'm going to have to do this later. If I don't start studying for our math test, my mom said she's going to put a lock on my closet and throw away the key."

I gripped the phone as my stomach lurched to my throat. "Math test?" I repeated weakly.

"Oh, Tessa, you forgot?" Mei sighed.

It was all coming back to me now. Ms. Webster's announcement last Friday about the first algebra test of the semester, the bobby pin I'd worn on Sunday to remind me to study, and the moment I'd forgotten about the bobby pin *and* the test when I was dreaming up the recipe for my bacon-peanut-butter cookies.

"I have to go," I said, and before Mei could utter another word, I was hanging up and hurrying out of my room.

"Mom," I said when I found her cleaning up the dinner dishes. "Can you take me to school? I left something important in my locker."

Her face fell, and I knew what was coming. "Tessa. Again?" There they were. The two words she said every time I forgot something at school, which I did at least once a week. She sighed and grabbed her car keys off the counter. "Okay, let's go."

The ride to and from school was blessedly silent. And, thankfully, the nighttime janitor was still there and heard my desperate knocking. But when we pulled into our driveway with my math book on my lap, Mom turned off the car and swiveled to face me in her seat. I braced myself for the responsibility lecture.

"This was one time too many, Tessa," she said quietly. "You agreed that you'd try harder to keep track of your assignments and test dates."

"I know, Mom," I said. "And I've *been* trying. . . ."

"It doesn't seem that way," Mom said. "It's the second week of the new semester and we're back to where we were before the break." She leaned against her headrest, closing her eyes like what she was about to say next pained her. "Maybe it's best that Flavorfest got canceled."

"What?" I said, not wanting to believe I'd heard her right.

"It might be good for you to spend less time at the truck," she said slowly. "I know you enjoy your time with Cleo, but I'm afraid that your schoolwork is getting compromised."

"It is not!" I said. "I got all A's and B's last semester. And I'm going to ace this test tomorrow, too!"

Mom opened her mouth in horror. "Your math test is *tomorrow*?"

I shriveled into the seat. I had failed to mention that earlier. "Yes, but —"

"You're going to be up all night studying!" Mom threw up her hands. "That's it, Tessa, no working at the truck for the rest of this week. I want you focusing on your schoolwork. And after this week, we'll see. . . ."

"You can't do that, Mom!" I cried. "Cleo needs extra help right now, and —"

"Cleo has Gabe and your friend Asher to help. She'll be fine."

"You're just doing this because you hate the Tasty Truck. You thought it was stupid for Cleo and Gabe to open it in the first place." Tears were burning the corners of my eyes now. "You hate that I love working there! You wish I loved numbers instead of cooking, just like you."

Mom looked stricken. "No, I don't. I —"

"What do you care if I spend all my time at the Tasty Truck?" I screamed, getting out of the car. "You never stop working long enough to notice where I am anyway."

Mom opened her mouth to say something else, but I slammed the car door and ran inside before I could hear her.

Cleo once told me that crying a few tears into your cooking brings joy to the people who eat the meal. Well, I cried gobs of tears into the last two bacon-peanut-butter cookies as I ate them, but I didn't feel one smidge of joy. Then again, maybe it doesn't work on the person who cooks the meal. I'd have to ask her when I got to the Tasty Truck tomorrow after school.

Then I remembered there would be no Tasty Truck after school tomorrow, and that made me cry harder. Finally, when I'd run out of tears, I wearily opened my math book to start studying. Even though I don't like math, I'm actually pretty good at it. Mom must've passed me at least a partial math gene somehow. By the time I drifted to sleep with my face plastered to an $a+b=c$ equation, I felt pretty good about the test, but horrible about everything else.

I might've dreamed it, but sometime in the middle of the night, I felt a cool hand press gently against my cheek, wiping away my tears.

# chapter
# seven

At lunch the next day, Mei all but pounced on me. "How'd the math test go?" she demanded.

"I think I only missed two," I said, stifling a yawn.

Mei burst into a happy dance in the cafeteria. "Yes!" she said. "That means you're still coming to the concert with us on Saturday night."

"It doesn't mean a thing until I do some big-time groveling," I said. "I haven't even told Mom and Dad about the concert yet, and considering Mom and I aren't speaking, that's going to be a little tricky."

"Come on, Tessa," Mei pleaded. "Talk to your mom. For me. Please."

*If* I aced my test, and *if* I cleaned my room so it looked more organized, and *if* I made a big show of doing my homework at the kitchen table all week long, I might have a chance at going to the concert. But those were some mammoth *if*s. And the last thing I wanted to do was ask Mom for a favor when I wanted to stay mad at her, oh, say, for the rest of my life.

Still, I heard myself say resignedly, "I'll talk to her. But it's going to take a lot for her to say yes."

This is what it took for Mom to say yes: one miraculous A-minus on my math test, two hours at the kitchen table every night doing homework (or, doing homework for the first hour and spending the second hour jotting down ideas for new recipes in my binder), one painful Wednesday afternoon organizing my room (by conveniently shoving most of my papers from last semester into the back of my closet), and one extremely lengthy groveling session in which I vowed never to forget another homework assignment ever again (except the latest spelling list that was currently MIA that she didn't know about).

By Friday afternoon, she'd agreed to the concert. I still felt the weight of our fight between us, though, like a thick San Fran fog that wouldn't lift.

"I want you to spend time with your friends," Mom told me. "But . . . Dad and I are still thinking about whether or not you can go back to work at the Tasty Truck."

When I started to protest, Mom held up her hand. "We'll make our decision by Sunday night."

Even Cleo couldn't come to my rescue this time.

"This is between you and your folks," she said to me when I begged her to try talking to them. "You know I love having you at the truck with me, but I can't get involved with this one."

I didn't push her, because ever since the city council meeting, she looked worn out. I'd overheard Dad giving her some ideas for how to cut back on spending, so it didn't sound like the Tasty Truck was doing any better. I was also worried that, without my help, working at the truck was tough on her. She told me that everything was fine, though.

"Asher's doing great," she said. "He's becoming a real pro."

At the sound of Asher's name, my stomach jumped. He and Tristan had stopped by my locker earlier in the week.

"Cleo told us what happened," Asher had said. "It stinks."

"Mostly it's his BLTs that stink," Tristan added. "They don't have the magic Tessa touch." He ruffled my hair, and the instant he did, I felt Asher's eyes on my face, gauging my reaction.

"I'll make you a double when I get back next week." I smiled self-consciously.

When I glanced at Asher, he was looking from me to Tristan thoughtfully, with the slightest frown on his lips. "So . . ." he began quietly. "*Will* you be back?" His voice rose hopefully in a way that made my breath catch.

"I'm planning on it," I said resolutely, then elbowed him. "Don't tell me you miss me harassing you about your sandwich-making skills."

"Not really." He grinned. "Mostly I just miss you doing all the work while I pretend to work. I can't get away with that when Cleo's around."

"Good," I said. "Maybe I shouldn't come back, then."

"Nah," he said. "There's a mob of disgruntled customers anxiously awaiting your return. I'd hate to disappoint them."

But as he walked away with Tristan, I found myself wondering if *Asher* would be disappointed if I didn't come back. I realized it wasn't only the Tasty Truck and Cleo that I missed. I'd actually started to enjoy working with Asher. My afternoons were just way too quiet without an argument or two with Asher to liven things up.

On Saturday, from the moment Mei's parents dropped us off at the Rickshaw Stop, Mei and Ben were a dynamic duo of snuggliness. They wouldn't let go of each other's hands even long enough to walk down the theater aisle, so other kids had to press against the wall to squeeze around them.

"So, which band's opening?" I asked as we took our seats.

"Huh?" Mei said without looking my way. "Oh, I don't know. Check the program."

I flipped through the program and a wrenching feeling of third-wheel-ness swept over me. Here I was, sitting next to my best friend, and suddenly I didn't know how to act around her. She wasn't herself anymore; she had become a clingy, giggly Ben magnet.

Luckily, the Young Sliderz took the stage and everyone was on their feet, screaming and clapping as the opening notes to "School Daze" pulsed through the theater. I started dancing alongside Mei and Ben. When the chorus came, Mei grabbed my hands and we belted out the lyrics together in between laughs.

For one split second, I almost forgot that Ben was there. But then Ben put his arm around Mei's shoulder and she was gone again, singing in his ear and swaying with him in time to the beat. I tried not to care and let myself get lost in the music, screaming out the words to the songs and with them, all the frustration I'd felt over the last week — at Mom, Mei, Asher, Karrie, Tristan, Mr. Morgan, everyone.

At one point, Mei tapped me on the shoulder and yelled something about going to get a soda in the lobby with Ben. I nodded distractedly and then went right back to dancing. I threw back my head and closed my eyes —

And someone slammed into me.

I felt the sickening sensation of my glasses flying off my face. Instantly, I was on my knees, feeling blindly in the dark around my seat, hoping they hadn't gone far. I found nothing but the sticky remnants of spilled soda and popcorn bits. I glanced around helplessly, but my close-up vision was a complete blur.

With frazzled nerves, I made my way out to the lobby to look for Mei and Ben, but I couldn't see them anywhere. I couldn't see the buttons on my cell well enough to text Mei, either. I wondered then if they'd found a corner somewhere in the theater for that kiss Mei had been wishing for, and my throat tightened.

Mei's mom had given us strict instructions on where to meet her outside the theater the second the concert was over. I knew Mei's parents were having dinner just around the block, but I couldn't for the life of me remember the name of the restaurant. This time of night, droves of tourists and San Franciscans came to Japantown to eat sushi and snap photos in front of the concrete pagoda. I knew my parents would kill me if I went roaming blindly through the packed streets trying to find Mei's parents.

I resigned myself to the inevitable and started to blindly dial Mom's cell, but then I heard someone call my name. I squinted at the fuzzy face in front of me, then felt a wave of relief as it gradually crystallized into a smiling Asher.

"What are you doing here?" he asked.

"Foodies are allowed to love music, too, you know," I said.

"Wow," he said. "I thought that was you, but . . ." He tilted his head, then looked surprised and bashful all at once. "You look so different."

"Oh." I patted my face. "Yeah. I lost my glasses in there."

He kept staring. "I've never seen you without them on. Your eyes . . . they're an amazing green."

I blushed furiously as my heart jumped. I had no idea what to say. Was Asher really complimenting me?

"Th-thanks," I stammered. "Too bad I can't really see much right now."

"Do you want to go back inside?" he asked, nodding toward the theater doors. "I can help you look for your glasses."

I gave a short laugh. "There's probably not much left of them. And I'm not really in the mood for the concert anymore."

"Yeah," he said. "Me either. I didn't really want to come in the first place, but Tristan and Karrie really wanted to, so . . ."

"You caved," I said.

"No," he said defensively. "I did the 'good friend' thing."

"Yeah," I said, easing off as I realized I'd basically done the same thing. "I came because Mei asked me to, but then she and Ben disappeared. I'm not even sure they remember I'm here."

"Sorry," Asher said, and I could tell by his voice that he meant it.

I held up my phone. "I was just about to call my mom to come get me. Do you need a ride home?"

He shook his head. "My mom's outside already. I told Tristan and Karrie I was leaving a few minutes ago. There's something else going on tonight that I finally decided wasn't worth missing." He hesitated, then added, "Hey, do you want to come over to my house to see it? It won't be around again for a while, and I think you'd like it."

My heart sped up and I gave it a mild, silent scolding. I so needed to get a grip. "Um, I'll have to check with my mom," I said. "But if she says it's okay, then I guess so." I took a step toward what I thought was the direction of the door, and bumped into the wall.

Asher laughed. "Need a little help?"

I shrugged and smiled in his general direction. "Maybe."

"Come here," he said, and before I could argue, he'd slipped his arm around my waist.

I caught my breath as heat jolted through me. I'd never been this close to any boy before. Thank goodness his face was a blur right now, or I would've been reminded how cute he was, and then I really would've been in trouble.

After a lengthy phone chat during which Mrs. Rivers assured her repeatedly that Asher and I would be under parental supervision at all times, Mom agreed to let me go over to Asher's. But she still said she'd pick me up by nine P.M. sharp.

"I'll call Mei's mom to let her know you're okay," Mom told me before we hung up. "I'm sure you and Mei just got separated in the crowd, that's all."

Or, Mei was too busy getting her first kiss to remember I was there.

I didn't want to think about Mei anymore tonight. Instead, I looked out the window of Mrs. Rivers's car as we made our way into the streets of the Presidio, with its jaw-dropping views of the bay and the Golden Gate Bridge. Most of the Presidio was a protected national park. My parents and I had walked through its beautiful grounds plenty of times, but I'd never been inside any of its amazing homes before.

Asher's apartment was almost as beautiful inside as the park was outside. An enormous glass wall stretched across the entire length of the living room, opening up to a view of the shimmering ocean below.

"Should I take off my shoes?" I whispered, but Asher just laughed.

"Come on," he said. "We have to go outside to see the show."

"Show?" I repeated. "Am I even going to be able to see this show without my glasses?"

"You're farsighted," he said. "It won't be a problem."

He led me out onto the terrace, which had a gorgeous pool and cabana-style lounge chairs.

"Hang on," he said, "I forgot to get the lights."

I wondered what he meant until he went inside and flipped off all of the pool and deck lights, plunging the terrace into darkness.

"Asher?" I called hesitantly. "I can't see."

Then I felt the lightest flutter of his hand on my back, and he whispered, "Okay . . . look up."

And there they were: streams of shooting stars pouring down from the sky. I'd never seen anything so magical.

"There are so many of them." I gasped. "Like it's raining stars."

"It's a meteor shower," Asher said. "One of the biggest ones we've had in over a century. This one comes every year and starts from a point right around the Big Dipper. That's called its radiant point." He leaned closer to me. "Can you see it?"

"It's incredible," I said, smiling.

"Yeah," he said. We were both quiet for a minute, and then he added, "After my parents got divorced, it felt strange in the house without my dad around. So Mom bought me a telescope and I started coming out here, just to get a break sometimes."

"It must've been tough," I said. "My parents are gone a lot, but at least they get along."

Asher nodded. "Mom's been lonely for a while, but she's dating again now, which is a little weird. But also better, because she's happier." He pointed to the telescope in the far corner of the deck. "Do you want to see more? Maybe we can try to find Venus or Jupiter." Then he hesitated. "But only if you want to . . ."

"I do," I blurted faster than I'd meant to. "I'm kind of glad that Mei and Ben disappeared tonight. I mean, I'm still furious at them for basically ditching me, but I would've hated to miss this." I gulped. It was the truth, but I couldn't believe I'd actually said it out loud. Still, when I risked a look at Asher and saw his blurry grin, I was glad I had. I was surprised at how good I felt about making him smile like that.

We were still bent over the telescope looking for the Horsehead Nebula when Mrs. Rivers came out onto the terrace to say Mom had come to pick me up.

I reluctantly said good night to Asher and got in Mom's car. On the way home, I told myself that what had happened tonight was a nonevent, just two friends hanging out. After all, this was Asher, the spoiled popular boy I could never seem to stop arguing with. But tonight, we hadn't argued. He'd been sweet and kind. And my humming pulse and swirling head told me that this might be the start of something new between us. But what it was, exactly, was as mysterious and uncertain as the night sky.

# chapter
# eight

I woke up the next morning to the warm, doughy smell of fresh baking. I tiptoed past Mom and Dad's closed door and up the stairs to Cleo's, squinting at the still-blurry world. I found Cleo in her kitchen, adding one last cinnamon roll to a heaping pile.

"I made breakfast for everybody!" she told me.

"Or . . . breakfast for the entire city?" I teased, pointing to the steaming omelets, pancakes, and fruit salad spread out on her kitchen counter.

Cleo shrugged. "So . . . I went a little overboard. I couldn't sleep." She motioned to a stack of papers scattered over her kitchen table. "I've been looking over the sales for the Tasty Truck." She sighed. "They've actually gone down over the last couple of months."

"Huh," I said. "Well, maybe it's been that way for all the truckers."

Cleo shook her head. "I've been talking to them." She bit her lip, staring forlornly at the papers. "It's our truck, Tessa. The other trucks are all doing better than we are, and I can't for the life of me figure out why. And now with no Flavorfest, I don't know how we're going to break out of this slump."

I felt the first stirrings of an idea. "Well, maybe there's a way we can still bring Flavorfest back. We just need to fight for it. . . ." Suddenly, I had a vision of Ansel Adams and the apartments he'd pasted in his photo of the Golden Gate hillsides. If he could fight for what was right through his art, then I could do it through my food. I snapped my fingers. "I know what we should do! We need to have a Save Flavorfest rally. Our own little protest against Mr. Morgan's Taste of San Fran. We can get everyone involved. Our neighborhood, the school . . . maybe the whole city! We can have it at the Tasty Truck and give away samples of our Bacon Me Crazy BLT to anyone who comes. It'll be perfect!"

A flicker of hope lit up Cleo's eyes. "If we can get the word out to all the food truckers, they'll spread the word to their customers. . . ." She bit into a piece of toast and chewed thoughtfully.

"We can have it next Saturday!" I said. "That'll give us a week to get everyone on board."

Cleo nodded, grinning, and I saw some of her spunk returning. Then her face fell. "But, Tessa, your mom and dad still haven't said yes to you coming back to work. They might not be happy about you getting involved in something like this. . . ."

My heart sank. In all my excitement, I hadn't even thought about that. "Well, maybe we don't have to tell them about the rally?" My voice was pleading. "Mom's flying to New York Tuesday morning on business and she won't be back until Saturday, and Dad's busy at a conference downtown this week, so we won't even really have to lie. We can just, I don't know, forget to mention it."

"That's a big thing to forget," Cleo said hesitantly. "They'll be upset if they find out, especially your mom. She told me the other night that she wanted to build more 'Tessa time' into her schedule."

"Really?" I asked, surprised. I often felt like I fell at the bottom of Mom's priority list. "Well," I said, "there won't be any openings in her schedule this week, not with her thousands of miles away." There was a hint of sarcasm in my tone, and Cleo picked up on it, frowning.

"Come on, Cleo," I persisted, "we can tell them about the rally after it's over."

"Okay," she said. "We won't mention it . . . *for now*. But they still have to agree to you coming back to work before you start helping me with the rally. I'm not budging on that."

"I'll go ask them right now," I said, already hurrying toward the stairs.

"Wait!" Cleo held out the platters full of omelets and cinnamon rolls. "Take these with you. Bribery might help."

I laughed. "Good thinking."

Mom and Dad were stumbling bleary-eyed toward the coffee-maker when I flew into the room.

"Breakfast!" I said enthusiastically, waving Cleo's platters under their noses.

"Mmmm," Dad said. "Looks delish."

"Thanks, sweetie," Mom said, taking a cinnamon roll. Then she peered into my face, her brow creasing. "Hey, what happened at the concert? I know you didn't want to talk about it last night, but I'm sure it was just a misunderstanding of some kind with Mei. . . ."

I saw the concern on her face, and just like that, I spotted my chance. I let my expression droop listlessly. "I don't know," I said morosely. "I'm not sure Mei and I are friends anymore."

It wasn't really an exaggeration. Mei had texted me about ten times since the concert, but I hadn't responded. We had our report on Ansel Adams due on Wednesday, but maybe there was a way we could finish it without actually speaking. Because after what happened at the concert, I didn't want to talk to Mei. Not today. Not tomorrow. Possibly not ever again.

I didn't hide my sadness in front of my parents. "I know you're still deciding about letting me go back to work," I told Mom, "but I think it would really cheer me up after everything. . . ."

I knew I was tapping into a weak spot. Neither one of them had ever been great at handling these kinds of dramas, and Dad was already starting to look lost. He gave Mom a *help me* look, and I sensed that she was the deciding factor here. Mom stared at the table for a long time, her mouth bordering dangerously on a frown.

Finally, she sighed. "All right, but before you go back to work, we're getting you a new pair of glasses. You're not dicing anything until you can see well enough to keep the knife away from your fingers."

"Done," I said, and then, possessed by a sudden, inexplicable impulse, I blurted, "Actually, Mom, I was thinking I might try contacts."

I blushed as Mom and Dad gawked at me. Mom had suggested contacts before, but I'd always been adamantly against trying them . . . until now.

"Wow, what brought this on?" Dad asked. "A historic day. I'm calling the *Chronicle*."

"Funny, Dad." I elbowed him, then shrugged. "And I don't know what brought it on."

Of course, I argued with myself, it had nothing to do with how Asher had reacted when he'd seen me without my glasses. Nothing at all.

Mom looked enormously pleased. "Great! We'll go to the eye doctor first thing tomorrow morning. Then you can help Cleo tomorrow afternoon at the truck." Her face grew more serious. "But no more midnight runs to school. I mean it, Tessa. You have to show me that you can work at the Tasty Truck *and* keep up with school, or we'll change our minds."

"I will," I said, beaming. "Thanks, Mom." Then I jumped up from the table and rushed to my room to call Mei. I was already halfway through dialing her number when I remembered what had happened last night. There was only one other person I could think of that I wanted to talk to, and with a hammering heart, I dialed his number.

I expected Asher to be thrilled about the idea for the rally. But when I told him about our plan, I was surprised by the silence I heard stretching out on the other end of the line.

"It's a great idea," he finally said, weakly. "I just don't think it's going to work."

"It might," I said. "Cleo told me this morning that the Tasty Truck's in real trouble, and I can't just sit back and wait for it to go under. We have to stop that from happening."

"And you really think Flavorfest will be enough?"

"It has to be," I said firmly. "If Flavorfest happens and the Bacon Me Crazy BLT wins, then the Tasty Truck will stay in business."

"So . . . what are you going to do?" he asked, and I wondered why he sounded so reluctant.

"I'm going to make a bunch a flyers and hand them out around our neighborhood," I explained. "I was hoping you could help me. Maybe we can start after we're done at the Tasty Truck tomorrow?"

"Sure," Asher said. Then there was a pause. "Tessa, no matter what happens, just try to remember that we're friends, okay?"

*Friends.* My heart involuntarily drooped a bit. "Of course we're friends," I said nonchalantly. "Nothing will change that."

"Good," he said, and the relief in his voice came through loud and clear.

After we hung up, I lay on my bed, the excitement I'd felt earlier deflating.

Of course that's what Asher and I were: friends. But why did he have to say it like I might need a reminder of that? Had he sensed something between us last night, too, or was he afraid that I felt something that he didn't?

I sighed, wondering why no one had ever invented an easy-to-follow recipe for boys. But then I knew the answer. Because no one understood boys well enough to write one.

On Monday, I missed my morning classes because I was at the eye doctor getting fitted for my very first pair of contacts. I was still getting used to the feel of them as I walked to my locker before lunch.

I spotted Mei there, waiting. I fleetingly hoped she might be about to apologize for what happened at the concert, but instead she narrowed her eyes.

"Where have you been for the last two days?" she demanded. "I tried texting you and calling you about a dozen times. I was worried something happened to you."

"That's a shocker." I stared at her. "You didn't seem too worried about me when you left me at the concert on Saturday."

Mei's eyes widened. "I didn't leave you. . . ."

"Right," I said. "You were gone for half an hour getting sodas!" I threw my books in my locker and slammed it shut.

"Why didn't you just wait for us?" Mei cried. "When we got back to our seats you were gone."

"Because my glasses got knocked off during the show, and I couldn't see a thing. I needed help, but you were oblivious to everything but Ben, as usual."

"What do you mean, 'as usual'?"

All my frustrations finally boiled over. "I mean that you're always with Ben, or thinking about Ben, or talking about Ben!" I cried. "It's completely awkward hanging out with you guys. I did almost all of the work on our Ansel Adams project because you were too busy helping Ben with his project. I tried to help you out by going to the concert with you but then you forgot I was there!" I let out an angry breath. "I'm just . . . sick of it!"

Mei's cheeks flashed red. "Fine. If you're so sick of it then I don't have to worry about going to the Great Pillow Fight with you this year."

"What?" I asked, my stomach plummeting.

Mei nodded. "Ben just asked me to go to the Sweet Heart Ball with him and I said yes. I didn't really want to go to the pillow fight anyway, but I didn't know how to tell you without hurting your feelings. But the truth is . . . I *hate* getting feathers in my mouth and I *hate* getting whacked with pillows. It used to be fun when we were about ten. Now I think the whole thing is . . . is stupid!"

I bit my lip to keep it from quivering. I'd always thought Mei had liked the pillow fight as much as I did. And now she was calling it stupid. The word cut deep, and made me think that maybe I didn't know as much about her as I thought I did. Maybe I didn't know her at all anymore.

"Whatever," I said, hoping she couldn't hear the tremor in my voice. "I don't want you to come with me anyway!" I started to walk away, then turned back. "Oh, and don't worry about the Ansel Adams project. I'll finish the rest of it myself."

I barreled down the hallway, hoping to make it to the girls' bathroom before anyone else saw the tears in my eyes. And then I realized something: Mei, the one person who'd always noticed everything about me, who'd been begging me to ditch my glasses forever, hadn't even noticed my new contacts. And for some reason, that made me feel worse than all the awful things my former best friend and I had said to each other.

It was a relief to return to the familiar sight of the Tasty Truck after school. But when I arrived, I saw Asher, Tristan, and Karrie and some of her girlfriends standing on the sidewalk. Tristan and Asher were finishing off the last bites of some BLTs while Karrie looked on in obvious distaste.

"Whoa," Tristan said when I walked over, "did you get contacts?"

I nodded, pleased that at least someone had noticed the change.

"It's a good look!" Tristan said. "Right, Ash?"

Karrie's eyes zeroed in on Asher, as if she was dying to hear what he'd say.

"Um . . . I guess," he said hesitantly, barely glancing at me. I remembered how he'd complimented my eyes on Saturday night and I didn't know *what* to think.

"On the other hand," Karrie quipped, a smile playing on her lips, "I heard glasses can really make a plain face pop. It was in a fashion magazine." She shrugged. "I doubt you read it."

I cringed as Karrie's pack snickered around her.

Karrie tapped her foot impatiently. "Can we go now, please?" she asked Tristan. She didn't wait for a response before starting to walk away with the other girls. "Asher, we'll see you later, too, unless you're planning on pulling a disappearing act again."

When they were gone, I turned to Asher. "What's with Karrie? I mean, she's never Miss Sunshine, but she's breaking new records today."

Asher shrugged as he opened the back door of the truck. "She's mad because I didn't stay for the whole concert on Saturday."

"Why does she care?" I said. "She had all her other friends there."

"Tristan told her that you ended up coming over to my place, and I guess she thinks . . ." His voice died away, and then his mocha skin darkened to *raspberry* mocha.

"Oh," I said quietly as understanding dawned on me. So Karrie liked Asher. And now Karrie thought that, what, Asher liked me? But, then, did Asher like Karrie, too?

The question was right there on my tongue, but the discomfort in Asher's face held me back. It didn't seem like something he wanted to talk about, and even though part of me wanted to ask him how he felt about Karrie, a bigger part of me was scared that his answer wouldn't be what I wanted to hear.

"I know, it's ridiculous," Asher said now, laughing nervously. "She's jumping to all these conclusions and she doesn't understand how it is with us."

"Of course she doesn't," I said, making my voice nonchalant even as my insides shriveled. What alternate reality did I think I was living in, anyway? Outside of the Tasty Truck, Asher and I existed in completely different social spheres. We could never be anything *more* than friends, no matter what my heart thought it wanted.

As we entered the truck, I put my disappointment on the back burner. I needed to focus on working *with* Asher instead of getting worked up *over* Asher.

In the last week while I was gone, Asher had become a pro. I didn't have to remind him to check the supplies of fresh veggies in the cold line, and the minute we ran low on anything he was on top of it, dicing up tomatoes or making a run to Cleo's rooftop for more herbs. I had to say, I was impressed.

After we closed up, Asher came over to help make the rally flyers. We worked side by side on the big computer in Mom's office,
and I was almost able to forget about my awful fight with
Mei, and whether or not Asher liked Karrie.

Finally, we had a hefty batch of flyers printed, and they looked
great.

I slid them into my backpack and carefully zipped it, making
sure they were out of Mom's sight. When I stood up to stretch,
my stomach growled embarrassingly.

Asher laughed, and suddenly some of the tension between us
eased a bit. "Hungry?" he asked with a smile.

"Starved," I said. "I can make us something. . . ." I started,
heading toward the kitchen.

"No!" Asher blurted. Then he gave a bow and added,
"Allow me."

I raised an eyebrow at him. "You're going to make *me*
something?"

"A Cassiopita," he said.

"A Cassiopita?" I asked.

Asher grinned slyly. "I made one in the truck last week, and then we tried it out on a few customers. They loved it."

I laughed at his pleased-as-punch look. "All right, sandwich pro, tell me what the ingredients are."

He rattled off the list and I handed him everything from the fridge and pantry. When it was all laid out on the counter, he waved his hand at me.

"Step aside, amateur, and let the expert show you how it's done." He swiftly piled jalapeño peppers, bacon strips, maple syrup, and diced chicken on a pita, then deftly wrapped it and handed it to me. He smiled satisfactorily. "And *that's* a Cassiopita."

"You learned a lot while I was gone," I said appreciatively.

He grinned. "That's because I could work without *somebody* breathing down my neck all the time," he teased.

"I was trying to help you," I said, sniffing indignantly.

"All right, all right. Now stop arguing with me and eat."

I lifted the sandwich to my lips and took a big bite.

"So . . . what do you think?" he asked.

"Hmmm," I said. "Maybe a *little* room for improvement here and there, but . . ."

He grabbed me in a playful headlock. "Are you kidding me? It took me three days to figure out that recipe. . . ."

I shrieked and ducked out from under his arm, tossing a handful of jalapeños at him.

"Oh, you're in trouble now," he said, launching some bacon missiles my way. Soon we were waging a full-on food fight, laughing hysterically at each bull's-eye. Finally, Asher caught me around the waist, holding the syrup threateningly over my head. "Admit you like my cooking," he said.

"Okay, okay, mercy." I gasped between giggles. "It's good! And I think we should put the Cassiopita on the menu for Flavorfest."

Just then, we heard the front door open. "Tessa?" Mom called, coming into the kitchen. "Are you —"

She froze mid-step, surveying the disastrous kitchen, littered with globs of syrup and spilled jalapeños. "What happened?" she breathed.

"Sorry, Mom," I said quickly, my face burning as Asher and I sprung apart. "We were just making sandwiches."

"Yeah," Asher said. "And getting ready for the ra —"

"Ready for the rush!" I jumped in. "Cleo wanted us to do some prep work for tomorrow's after-school rush, that's all."

Asher shot me a questioning glance, but Mom sighed.

"Well, just clean up, okay?" she said as she passed through the kitchen, heading for her office. Then she paused to give me one of her no-nonsense looks. "And make sure you stay on top of your schoolwork, like we talked about."

I nodded. Once Mom had disappeared into her office, Asher and I quietly cleaned everything up. Then I walked him to the front door to wait for his mom to pick him up.

"So," he said, "your mom doesn't know about the rally?"

I shook my head. "I don't think I'm going to tell her."

"Why not?"

I stared at the floor. "Because she won't get it. She'd probably tell me it was a bad idea to stir things up, and that I shouldn't be focusing on a ridiculous rally when school comes first."

"How do you know she'd say that?"

"Because those are the kinds of things she always says."
I shrugged. "To her, cooking is a big waste of my time."

Asher looked at me for a minute. "Maybe you just need to give her a chance. She might surprise you."

I laughed. "My mom isn't programmed for surprises."

Asher's mom pulled up outside the window then, and he shouldered his backpack. "It was fun today . . . working together." He smiled at me. "We make a pretty good team when you're not being a know-it-all."

"And when you're not being a snob." I laughed. "I'll bring the flyers to school tomorrow, bright and early."

"I'll be there," he said, bouncing down the stairs. Then on the bottom step, he turned around. "And I *do* like your new contacts. A lot."

I waited, smiling in the doorway, until his car was gone. Somehow, the day that had started off so badly was finishing better than I'd ever expected.

# chapter
# nine

The next morning, when I saw Tristan was waiting for me alone at my locker, my stomach twisted nervously.

"Hey," I said. "Where's Asher?"

"He called," Tristan said. "They're stuck in traffic, but he'll be here soon." He nodded toward my bulging backpack. "You're going to hang up some flyers?"

"Yep. As long as there's some space in between all the flyers for the Sweet Heart Ball." I thought of Mei and my throat tightened.

Tristan raised his eyebrows at my snarky tone. "You're not so into the ball?"

I shook my head. "I'm not planning on going."

"Really?" He sounded surprised. "So . . . nobody's asked you yet?"

"Um, no," I faltered. My heart starting hammering in panic, and suddenly I couldn't meet his eyes. Was Tristan about to ask me to the dance? I was so unprepared to deal with that right now, on top of everything else.

Most girls would jump for joy if Tristan asked them to the Valentine's Day dance. But I suddenly knew with absolute and total certainty that I could never go to the dance with him. Tristan was great, but there was only one person I wanted to go with.

But after our talk yesterday afternoon, I knew Asher would never ask me.

"If the right guy asked you, though," Tristan was saying, dropping his voice, "would you go?"

"U-um," I stuttered. This was über-awkward. Was Tristan

hinting that *he* was the right guy? "Tristan, there just . . . isn't a right guy right now."

"Oh," Tristan said, "because I wanted to ask you if . . ."

I closed my eyes, praying he wouldn't finish. And miraculously he didn't, and when I tentatively opened one eye, I saw why. Asher was coming down the hallway toward us.

I let out the breath I'd been holding. All I could do now was hope that Tristan had somehow gotten the message and would never, ever try to ask again.

"Did you bring them?" Asher asked as I struggled to pull myself together enough to actually meet his gaze.

I nodded, trying to forget what had just happened with Tristan. I pulled a stack of flyers out of my backpack. They all read:

## Save Flavorfest!

Food truckers, bacon lovers, and neighbors unite! The fate of our great city's food trucks rests in your hands. Meet at the Tasty Truck on Saturday, February 1st, at noon, to show your support for Flavorfest. Bring your family, friends, and fighting spirit. We're giving away samples of our Flavorfest

Best-nominated BLT to anyone who stops by. We are the voice of the community, and we can save Flavorfest!

"Free BLTs," Tristan said, patting his stomach. "Count me in." Then he waved to us and ambled off down the hall, acting as if our whole weird exchange had never happened.

"Come on," Asher said. "Let's go get permission from Principal Keeler to hang up the flyers."

Luckily, our principal turned out to be an easy convert.

"Your aunt's Bacon Me Crazy BLT is up for the Flavorfest Best Award?" he asked me as he scanned the flyer. "I *love* that sandwich. I walk down to the truck for lunch twice a week! I'd go every day if my wife would let me, but she's worried about my cholesterol, so on Tuesdays and Thursdays it's tofu instead."

"I . . . didn't know that," I said, glad that he was a fan but also slightly weirded out by this window into his personal life.

He handed me back the flyer, then said with conviction, "Go for it. Post them all over school. Save Flavorfest for the sake of your BLT."

Before the first bell, Asher and I had posted flyers on every bulletin board in the school and tucked them into the vents of nearly all the lockers.

I was just taping the second-to-last flyer onto the mirror in the girls' bathroom when Karrie came floating in on her cloud of holier-than-thou-ness.

"Oh," she said snottily, eyeing the flyer. "I saw Asher handing those out in the hallway, too. I hope he's getting paid overtime."

"Actually," I shot back, "he volunteered to help me."

Her face didn't betray any surprise, but I thought I saw her eyes narrow ever so slightly. "I didn't know he was starting to like his job so much. What a change of heart." She checked her reflection in the mirror. "I'll have to make sure he asks off for the afternoon of the Sweet Heart Ball. We'll be taking pictures early." She paused, studying my face. "Is something wrong, Tessa? You've gone all pasty."

"No!" I said instantly, forcing a smile onto my face even as my chest began to ache.

"Are you sure?" Her voice smacked of fake sympathy. "'Cause for a second there I thought maybe I was crushing your hopes about Asher or something. . . ."

My laugh came out sounding hollow. "That's crazy," I said. "I just didn't know that he'd asked you to the dance. That's all."

"He hasn't yet," she said. "But I'm sure he will."

The next words stuck in my throat until I finally forced them out. "Well, I hope it works out . . . if it's what Asher wants."

I was still reeling from Karrie's news when I sat down in art history. Mei walked into class holding one of my flyers. And if Mei had slapped me in the face right then and there, it wouldn't have hurt as much as watching her glance at the flyer, and then swiftly crumple it and toss it into the trash.

On our way to the Tasty Truck after school, Asher and I stopped at every food truck in Russian Hill. It was all I could do to keep the smile on my face as I hyped up our Flavorfest rally to anyone and everyone who would listen. I made myself go through the motions, even through my leaden glumness. It must've worked, too, because all the food-truck owners gave a resounding "Yes" to the rally.

"You're going to have an amazing turnout," Asher said as we approached the truck.

"Yeah," I said. "I guess everyone is on board, except for Mr. Morgan and . . ." I almost added *Mei*, but didn't, not wanting to put a damper on our success. But Asher, of course, saw right through me. I'd told him about my fight with Mei during our walk, and he'd listened sympathetically. It seemed hard to believe that just a few weeks ago, I'd hardly said two words to him, and now, talking to him came so naturally. Which only made it hurt more every time I thought of him asking Karrie to the dance.

"Hey," Asher said now, looking earnestly into my eyes. "Mei wasn't thinking when she trashed the flyer. You both need a chance to cool down, that's all. I bet she'll still come to the rally. A lot can change between now and Saturday."

"Thanks for saying that." I sighed. "But . . . I don't think so. She's too busy with Ben, and it's just not that important to her. Besides" — I shrugged — "I don't care if she comes or not."

Asher raised a skeptical eyebrow. "For the record, you're a lousy liar."

I let out a small laugh. "The truth is more my style, but it always seems to cause trouble. I was honest with Mei, and now we're not speaking to each other. When I'm honest with my mom about the Tasty Truck, we end up fighting. Maybe I should try lying more often."

"Nah," Asher said. "That's one of the things that's great about you. I wish I could be that honest all the time."

"You don't think you are?" I asked, wondering if maybe he was leading up to telling me about Karrie himself.

"I know I'm not. There are plenty of times I should tell people what I really think, but don't. Like, say, if there was a girl who liked me that I wasn't into . . ." His voice got quieter, more hesitant. "It wouldn't be fair to let her keep thinking that I might like her, right?"

"Right," I said, my stomach seizing. Maybe this was it. He was trying to set the record straight, once and for all, hinting that I shouldn't ever expect anything but friendship from him.

I took a deep breath, bracing myself. If Asher *was* trying to let me down easy, I had to take it all in stride, or we'd never be friends again.

"So, with this girl," I said, "you should be honest. Because the longer you lead her on, the more hurt she'll be when she finds out it wasn't real."

Asher seemed to think this over, then he nodded. "You're right. I need to tell her. I mean, we're already friends, so she'll understand, won't she?"

"Even if she doesn't want to, she'll have to," I said quietly, feeling a lump in my throat.

"So," Asher said, changing the subject, "what else do we need to do to prep for the rally?"

"Just keep spreading the word," I said halfheartedly. "I'm going to decorate the Tasty Truck with some banners on Friday night, if you want to help."

Asher's smile dimmed, and his face took on an uncomfortable, reluctant look.

"I mean, I don't want to pressure you or anything," I said, trying to undo whatever wrong turn I'd just taken. "You've helped a lot already, I just thought —"

"Sure, I'll help," he said. "There's just something . . ." His brow furrowed, but then we reached the truck, and he mumbled, "Never mind. It can wait."

"Guys!" I heard Cleo calling from the truck. She leaned out the window, holding up her cell phone. "Come look at this." Her face drained of color and was tight with tension.

"You're not going to believe this," she said in a doomsday voice as Asher and I hurried inside the truck.

"What?" I asked with dread.

Cleo pulled up YouTube on her cell, then handed it to me. "This was just posted a half hour ago, but it already has over a thousand hits."

I couldn't believe my eyes. The video on the screen showed Karrie, smiling gorgeously while simultaneously brushing tears away from her meticulously mascara-ed eyes. "It was so . . . so shocking," she was saying. "I mean, it was right there! A cockroach the size of a small rodent crawling across the floor of the Tasty Truck, in plain view. It gives new meaning to the words *roach coach*!" She sniffled. "The whole thing makes me so sad. I mean, Tessa goes to my school! I know her!" She heaved a sigh worthy of an Oscar-winning actress. "But after this, I don't think I can eat at her family's food truck ever again."

I looked up at Cleo in disbelief. "But — but she's never eaten anything at the Tasty Truck! Ever!" I cried, my blood boiling. My morning run-in with Karrie had been brutal enough. I'd never imagined anything like this.

"I know." Cleo nodded sympathetically. "It doesn't matter, though. She's already got the sound bite, *and* that dayglow smile to make everyone believe it."

"What are we going to do?" I asked her.

Cleo shrugged in a helpless, defeated way so unlike her that it made me go cold all over. "I don't know if there's anything we can do. There's no way to prove she didn't see a cockroach." She sighed. "With every hit that video gets, she's hurting our reputation."

"But it's only on YouTube," Asher said, looking painfully uncomfortable with the whole conversation. "It can't be that big of a deal."

"It's not . . . yet," Cleo said. "All we can do is wait and see what happens." She frowned, then headed for the door. "I have to get some supplies from the garden."

Asher and I settled into our routine, but now there was quiet tension in the truck with us. I wanted him to be furious with Karrie the way I was. I wanted to tell him what I was thinking, but I was afraid that he might defend Karrie, and I didn't think I could handle that.

When Cleo came back, she looked even more shaken up. "Gabe just texted me," she told us. "Karrie's video was on the local news. And so was Mr. Morgan, with a bunch of 'I told you so's' about dirty food trucks."

"Great." I slumped against the counter. "Somebody has to talk to Karrie and get her to tell the truth."

"She'll never do it." They were the first words Asher had spoken in ages. I glanced at him, and saw that he looked as sick about the whole thing as I felt.

"But we have to try —"

"I have to go," Asher said, grabbing his backpack from the storage closet. But he paused in the open door and turned to Cleo. "I'm sorry."

Then, before I could even say good-bye, he was gone.

chapter
# ten

Speaking in front of a roomful of people had never been a problem for me . . . until Wednesday morning in art history class. What complicated matters was the fact that the person I was supposed to be speaking *with* wasn't speaking *to me* at all.

"Ansel Adams was a great conservationist as well as a talented artist," I said, reading from the cue cards I'd written, "and his photographs of Yosemite and other national parks have helped protect them for decades."

This was supposed to be Mei's cue to launch the PowerPoint photo montage she had put together. But since we hadn't worked out those details, or spoken so much as one word to each other since our blowup on Monday, I had to clear my throat and nod in her direction to clue her in.

"Oh!" she blurted, then fumbled to start the program on Mr. Toulouse's laptop.

The rest of the presentation was just as discombobulated, with Mei and me blundering through in a series of out-of-order photos. When it was finally over, I collapsed into my seat with a huff. Out of the corner of my eye, I saw Mei hide her face in her hands, shaking her head in dismay.

As awkward as the presentation had been, I was relieved to have it over, at least until Mr. Toulouse called Mei and me up to his desk right after the bell rang.

Mr. Toulouse shifted his glance from Mei's face to mine, as if trying to piece together a puzzle.

"Girls," he finally said, "your presentation today was informative and met all of the project requirements, so I'm giving it a B-plus."

"Thank you," Mei and I unintentionally said together, then instantly stiffened.

Mr. Toulouse's eyebrows arched over the top of his glasses. "That being said, I couldn't help feeling that the pep and vigor I normally see from you two was sadly missing from your report." He rubbed his chin thoughtfully. "Is there anything the matter?"

"No!" Mei burst out, a little too eagerly. "Everything's fine."

"Just hunky-dory," I added with false spunk.

It was a flat-out lie, not just because of Mei, but because of Karrie's video. I'd heard whispers flying around the school hallways, and I guessed from the not-so-subtle glances kids were giving me that the rumor mill was having a heyday with Karrie's story.

I hadn't had a chance to talk to Asher about his running-scared routine yesterday. And because he had baseball practice after school today, I wouldn't see him at the truck, either.

"Well," Mr. Toulouse said now, "if you two say everything's all right, then I suppose I have to believe you." Then he leaned forward conspiratorially. "But I have to admit, I miss catching you writing notes to each other during class. First period isn't nearly as exciting when you're both so well-behaved."

I nodded meekly, then escaped out the door, with Mei close behind. But when we reached the hallway, we instantly separated, with Mei hurrying to where Ben was waiting at her locker. Ben glanced at me, shrugging apologetically.

*Good,* I thought. *He should feel bad, stealing away my best friend.* But as soon as I thought it, guilt washed over me. It wasn't entirely Ben's fault that Mei was forgetting me. I wasn't just afraid Mei was forgetting me for Ben, I was afraid she was outgrowing me altogether.

When I got to the Tasty Truck after school, Gabe's eyes were bulging bug-like with panic. He was staring helplessly at a pile of BLTs.

"Look at this," he said mournfully. "I made these a few hours ago, in preparation for the lunchtime rush, and they're still sitting here. The only things anyone has bought from us in the last four hours were sodas and water bottles. No fresh food."

"Maybe it's just a slow day," I said, trying to think of a logical explanation, aside from the one already nagging away at me.

"This is more than just a slow day." Cleo shook her head. "People are afraid to eat our food."

"But that's insane," I protested. "There's nothing wrong with our food."

"It doesn't matter," Cleo said in a resigned voice. "People believe what they see on the news, whether it's true or not. Two other trucks already got inspected by the Department of Health and Sanitation today. Of course they passed their inspections with flying colors, but that's not the point. If we don't stop this right now, we're going to start losing customers permanently. No one will come to the rally, and Flavorfest won't stand a chance."

A leaden weight settled over me. Suddenly, there was a loud throat-clearing in the direction of the truck window that made us all jump, and we glanced up to see a stern-looking man with a clipboard and a pocket protector.

"Can I help you?" Cleo asked.

"Dan Gervis," he said. "Department of Health and Sanitation. There's been a complaint filed with our department. I'm here to do an inspection."

I stared at him in disbelief. This could not be happening. But when Cleo smiled welcomingly and told Mr. Gervis to come right inside and make himself at home, I knew it was. And when I thought it couldn't possibly get any worse, it did. Because right as Mr. Gervis stepped into the truck, we heard a loud voice holler from outside the truck, "Hey. That's the roach coach we saw on the news last night!"

I looked out the window just in time to see a family of tourists happily snapping pictures of our Tasty Truck.

Mr. Gervis stiffened at the words, and I gripped the counter, a storm of fury rising inside me. In that moment, I was certain of one thing: I was never going to let Karrie get away with this.

I grabbed my backpack and motioned Gabe outside while Cleo chatted sweetly with the inspector.

"I'm going to try to fix this," I said. "But I need you to drive me to the baseball field right now."

Gabe nodded, grabbing his car keys. "If you can fix this, Tessa, I'd drive you to the moon."

I got to the field just as Tristan was walking off it.

"Hey, Tessa!" he said, giving me a smile that I tried desperately to interpret as just friendly and nothing more. "What are you doing here? Aren't you supposed to be at the Tasty Truck?"

"Where's Asher?" I asked.

"He just headed for the locker room," he said. "What's the matter?"

Our awkward moment about the dance was still fresh in my mind, but Karrie's latest coup trumped everything else.

"The Tasty Truck is under siege," I said. "Karrie's going to completely ruin our reputation."

"That's brutal," Tristan said sympathetically. "I can't believe it's getting blown that far out of proportion."

I nodded. "That's why I'm here. I came to see if you and Asher could talk to her. You're her friends. She'll listen to you guys. . . ."

Tristan shook his head. "Asher already tried talking to her about it last night. I guess he called her as soon as he found out."

"Oh," I said. So *that's* where he'd gone when he blew out of the Tasty Truck.

"She's sticking to her story," he said. "We know she's lying, but . . ."

"But what?" I stared at him. "Nobody has the guts to call her on it?"

"Saying she's a liar won't change anything," he said. "Most of the school already believes her. That's how she operates. She gets everyone into her camp and then no one challenges her."

"Why does she have such a vendetta against me?" I cried.

"I don't know," Tristan said. "There was your lip-gloss joke. And I think she's mad about Asher ditching her at the concert for you."

"But — but that's not what happened," I said. "He said he *wanted* to leave!"

Tristan shrugged. "Well, just be glad Asher's not coming to the rally, because if he were, she'd probably be even nastier."

My heart took a nosedive. "What did you just say?" I whispered, because I knew I couldn't possibly have heard him right the first time.

"Man, I'm sorry," Tristan said. "I thought you already knew. Asher's not coming to the rally."

I was halfway to the locker rooms before I even registered that Tristan was still standing in the middle of the baseball field, calling my name. But I couldn't stop. I didn't want to hear the excuses he was sure to have for Asher. No excuse could possibly be good enough.

Asher was coming out the gym door when he caught sight of me. His eyes met mine, and they widened in dread. He knew I'd just found out.

"What is wrong with you?" I cried. "You weren't going to even bother telling me that you weren't coming?"

He held up his palm like a peace flag. "Wait a sec, Tessa. It's not what you think. . . ."

"Really? And what do I think? That you can't come because your soon-to-be girlfriend wants to bring down the food truck?"

His face went creased into confusion. "Are you talking about Karrie?" He shook his head adamantly. "Sh-she's not . . ." he stammered. "That's . . . Argh! Would you just give me a chance to explain?"

I forced my mouth closed, then crossed my arms, glowering. "Fine," I muttered.

"I want to go to the rally. Honestly I do." He sighed. "But . . . I can't."

"Because Karrie doesn't want you to?" I challenged.

His brow knit in confusion. "No. Karrie doesn't have anything to do with it. And even if she didn't want me to go, that wouldn't stop me, especially after what she pulled yesterday." He paused. "No, I can't go because my *mom* doesn't want me to."

Now it was my turn to look confused. "What? But . . . why?"

He took a deep breath. "Because she's dating Mr. Morgan, that's why."

"What?" I was stunned. Mrs. Rivers was dating Mr. Morgan? "Why didn't you tell me?"

"I didn't make the connection between him and the Flavorfest at first. And then once I figured it out, I guess I just didn't think it was that big of a deal."

I gawked at him. "How could it not be a big deal? You know how much the Flavorfest meant to the Tasty Truck, and Cleo . . . and me."

"I know, but my mom is the one dating him, not me. It's not like I'm suddenly in Mr. Morgan's camp or anything. I didn't lie about it."

"No, but you didn't tell me the truth, either."

"Look, I just didn't see the point in stirring everything up. . . ." His voice died away and he stared at the floor, pulling his shoulders inward. "My mom really likes Mr. Morgan, and she's afraid that if I go to the rally, he'll get mad at her." He shrugged apologetically. "I know it sounds ridiculous. But Mom doesn't want the two of us getting off on the wrong foot. I think after what happened with my dad, she's worried about messing things up."

I was silent for a long time, my head spinning. It all seemed like too much to take in. "I can understand you not wanting to hurt your mom's feelings," I finally said. "I can even understand you not wanting to get on Mr. Morgan's bad side while your mom's dating him. But if the rally's something you really believe in, then *they* should understand that, too. Why don't you talk to your mom about it again? Maybe she'll change her mind."

Asher was already shaking his head. "No. It's just . . . easier this way."

"Easier for *you*, you mean," I said, my anger flaring up again. "You don't ever fight for anything. You can't even stand up to Karrie when you know she's lying about the Tasty Truck. You're embarrassed when your so-called friends say awful things, but you never stop them. If you don't fight for what you believe in, then how does anyone know who you really are?" I stared at him. "When you're done working at the Tasty Truck, will we still even be friends? Or will you just pass me in the hallways, pretending like it never even happened?"

"It won't be like that," he said.

"I don't know if I believe you," I said, biting my lower lip to keep it from trembling. "I don't know if I can trust anything you say."

I turned away swiftly and ran to Gabe's car.

"Let's go," I said, unable to hide the quiver in my voice as I climbed inside.

"Hey," Gabe said, looking worried. "Is everything okay?"

"Not even close," I managed to mumble. I pressed my forehead against the window. A raw, penetrating hurt gnawed into me, like when you trust yourself a little too much cooking with a hot skillet, and then you end up getting burned.

# chapter
## eleven

On Friday afternoon, I strung the last of the banners across the Tasty Truck, then stepped back to survey my work. The entire truck was draped in colorful signs blasting the words SAVE FLAVORFEST and LONG LIVE THE BLT! For this last banner, I'd painted an enormous BLT on one end and given it a bacon smile, a smile that felt completely wrong.

"That looks great," Cleo said. But her smile looked all wrong, too, like it was hurting her to wear it. She squeezed my hand. "Thanks, Tessa. No matter what happens tomorrow, I'm so glad we decided not to cancel the rally."

"I am, too," I said, but I wondered how much truth was behind those words.

Since Wednesday, our sales at the Tasty Truck had been dismal. Partly because things were so slow at the truck and partly because she knew that I'd had a huge fight with him, Cleo called Asher and told him she wouldn't need him at the truck on Thursday or Friday. Cleo told me that he'd stopped by the truck once on Thursday to buy a bunch of bacon-bits brownies, which had seemed strange, but luckily I'd been getting herbs from the garden and had missed him by a few minutes. I was relieved I didn't have to go through the awkwardness of seeing him, but it still didn't make what was happening to our truck any easier to take.

Five more food trucks in our neighborhood had gotten surprise inspections from Mr. Gervis, and even though every single one, including the Tasty Truck, had gotten five stars, the best ranking, it didn't matter. Sales were down for all of us. It was just like Cleo had predicted. People were afraid of our food. In fact, after sitting in the truck for three hours on Thursday without a single customer, Cleo decided to close the truck until the rally.

I wondered if the rally would really make a difference, though. We had no idea if anyone besides the other food-truck owners would come. At school this morning, Principal Keeler had been nice enough to remind everyone about the rally over the intercom during announcements. But I didn't have high hopes that anyone listened. Between Karrie's little video, and Mr. Morgan — who was probably going to be Asher's stepdad any day now — the damage had been done.

"Well," Cleo said as she checked over the stock of supplies in the truck one last time. "I guess that's all we can do for tonight. We'll make the BLTs tomorrow morning."

Our walk back to the house was silent. When we reached the front step, I could hear the phone ringing inside. Cleo hurried to open the door, and I scrambled to grab the phone.

"Hello?" I said.

"Tessa." It was Tristan's voice, and my heart lurched. Was he calling to pick up where we left off with our Valentine's Day conversation? Oh, I hoped not. If I had to have a *just-friends* talk with him right now, my already-frazzled nerves would fry. But, instead, what he said was, "Turn on Channel Seven right now. Hurry!"

I grabbed the remote and flipped to Channel Seven. I sank down on the couch in utter shock when Karrie's face appeared, larger than life on the screen. She was happily munching on one of the Tasty Truck's bacon-bits brownies.

"Mmmm, so good," she said, reaching for another one from the plate in front of her. "These are the best brownies I've ever had."

The screen switched to Bev Channing's face, and I could see she was struggling not to laugh as she said, "Karrie Lopes is issuing an apology to the Tasty Truck this evening after she was caught on video enjoying some Tasty Truck desserts. The video was taken *after* she lodged her supposed complaint, and it went viral on YouTube this morning. Now let's hear what she has to say."

The screen flickered to a miserable-looking Karrie, with her parents standing behind her in the background, just as miserable. "Yes, I lied earlier this week when I said I saw a cockroach in the Tasty Truck," Karrie said in a monotone. "There never was a cockroach." There was a pause, and her mother leaned forward and whispered something into Karrie's ear. "Oh, yes," Karrie added uncomfortably, "and I'm sorry for any harm my dishonesty caused the Tasty Truck . . . and its owners."

"Omigod!" I shrieked, leaping off the couch to hug Cleo, who'd been watching the news clip with her mouth hanging open. "That's amazing!" I said into the phone.

"I know," Tristan said. "I just uploaded the whole thing to Facebook and I'm sharing it with everyone at school."

"Thank you," I gushed. "How on earth did you manage to get that on video?"

"I didn't," Tristan said. "It was Asher."

"What?" I gasped, my heart jumping.

"I guess he took a bunch of your brownies over to her house and pretended he'd made them himself," Tristan said. "Then he called the news station with it." He laughed. "I've never seen Karrie break a sweat before. And on television, too. Priceless."

"No kidding." I giggled, my spirits lifting for the first time all week.

"Well, make lots of sandwiches for the rally tomorrow," Tristan said. "I have a feeling there's going to be quite a crowd after this."

"We will," I said, beaming. "Are you coming?"

"Absolutely," Tristan said. "There's no way I'd pass up free BLT samples." Then he added, as an afterthought, "And, of course, I'm fighting to save Flavorfest, too."

He said good-bye and I hung up the phone laughing. Suddenly, the world had turned right side up again, and I had Asher to thank for it.

The morning of the rally dawned chilly, drizzly, and foggy. But not even the gloomy weather could ruin my mood. This was it, the moment of truth, when we'd find out just how much the Tasty Truck and Flavorfest meant to the community. Maybe hundreds of people would come; maybe we'd make the evening news; maybe Mr. Morgan would crack under pressure. Maybe by the time the rally was over, Flavorfest would be back. It would be amazing . . . if it worked.

Last night, after Cleo and I had watched, and re-watched, laughed, and laughed some more at the video of Karrie gobbling up our brownies, I made as many signs and posters as I could.

I'd felt newly motivated, especially now that I knew Asher was on our side. I even had a faint sprig of hope that he might show up at the rally, in spite of his mom's relationship with Mr. Morgan.

Dad had gone to bed early, and I worked quietly in my room so he wouldn't hear what I was up to. He and Mom still didn't know about the rally, since Cleo, Gabe, and I had been careful to keep it under wraps. As far as they knew, Saturday was just a regular workday for us.

Now I glanced out the living room window to see Gabe pulling up to the curb with the Tasty Truck. The second I saw it decked out with its colorful banners, a surge of adrenaline rushed through me. I called to Cleo, and we hurried outside into the cool fog with our signs.

Soon, Gabe had pulled the truck up to the corner of Hyde and Lombard. The minutes ticked steadily by as we fired up the grill and churned out dozens of BLTs, making sure to add a healthy dollop of special sauce to each one before slicing them and wrapping them up into small, sample-sized portions.

By 11:55 A.M., our truck was fully stocked with BLT samples, sodas, water bottles, and everything else we'd need to get us through the rally. There was only one problem.

"No one's coming," I said, panicking as I looked up and down the length of the empty sidewalk.

"It's still early," Cleo said. "We have time."

But when another few minutes went by, even she started to look a little hopeless. I was seconds away from tossing my sign into the trash can and giving up when I heard it. A distant hum at first. A sound that slowly crystallized into voices, lots of them, all cheering and chanting excitedly.

I saw the huge crowd rounding the crest at the top of Lombard Street. Hope rose up in my chest. There were at least a hundred people, if not more, slowly weaving their way down the winding street, with Signor Antonio taking up the lead, grinning happily under his fedora.

"Flavorfest forever, Taste of San Fran never!" they shouted, pumping signs in the air to the rhythm of their chant.

"See?" Cleo said, beaming. "I knew they'd come."

I grinned, then grabbed my sign and raced up the hill to join the crowd. When Signor Antonio saw me, he tipped his hat.

"It's a fine day for a protest, Tessa," he said jokingly, pointing at the overcast sky. "Don't you think?"

I laughed. "I was afraid no one would come."

Signor Antonio waved his hand. "We are a community."

I glanced over his shoulder at an ocean of familiar faces. Nearly all of the food truckers in our neighborhood had come. There were the Bisratis, the Hirschorns, the Osakas. And they were all smiling encouragingly at me.

"Good work, Tessa," Mrs. Osaka said. "You brought us all together."

Mr. Bisrati nodded. "It was high time for us to speak up, and now we can do it with one voice."

"Thanks," I said, blushing.

I looked past them into the crowd, and spotted a bunch of kids from school. I instinctually looked for Mei, and then Asher. Even though I should have known better, disappointment seeped into my heart when I didn't see either of them. But then I caught sight of Tristan. He waved at me and held up a handmade sign that read: DON'T GO BACON MY HEART. SAVE FLAVORFEST FOR THE BLT'S SAKE!

"What do you think?" he hollered over the din of the crowd.

"I love it," I hollered back. Then I mouthed the one word I was afraid to say out loud. "Asher?"

Tristan shook his head almost imperceptibly, and I let go of the breath I'd been holding.

I'd so badly wanted Asher to come, mostly because I wanted to thank him for the Karrie video. And to apologize for second-guessing him. But I'd have to do that later.

Tristan pointed a finger at me now, and mouthed, "Can we talk later?"

*Gulp.* He just wasn't going to give up, was he? I sighed. Well, it wasn't fair to keep avoiding it, so I nodded at him, guessing I should get our talk over with. I liked Tristan; I just didn't *like* like him. But I hoped we'd still be friends once I told him that.

Tristan gave me a thumbs-up, and then Signor Antonio tipped his hat to me, bowing slightly. "*Per favore, signorina*, lead the way."

I glanced back at the crowd nervously, then thought of the Tasty Truck and found my courage. Taking a deep breath, I raised my sign in the air and shouted, "Come on everybody. Louder this time! Flavorfest forever, Taste of San Fran never! Flavorfest forever, Taste of San Fran never!"

Each time I said it, my spirits lifted higher and higher, and by the time we reached the Tasty Truck, I was convinced the entire universe could hear our message. We formed a broad oval in front of the truck and started marching with our signs. Slowly but surely, other people trickled in to join us. Apartment windows opened up and down the street, and curious folks popped their heads out to see what was going on, with some of them eventually joining in the chant. As the afternoon wore on, more and more people came, until most of the sidewalk on the block was taken up by the crowd. All of our regular customers stopped by to show support, and many brought friends and family with them. Even a few store owners on Hyde Street closed shop early to march alongside us.

At one point, I even had a surreal moment when I thought I saw a woman who looked like Mom on the outskirts of the crowd. She was hanging back, watching the marching. But just when I took a step toward her, a family of five stepped between us, wanting to order more sandwiches. By the time I'd helped Gabe with their order, the Mom look-alike had disappeared.

"I can't believe the turnout," Cleo said gleefully as she gave me another batch of BLT samples to hand out to the growing crowd. "I tell you, Tessa, this is what freedom of speech is all about. We're making history."

I laughed, knowing that Gabe and Cleo had done their fair share of protesting and picketing before. "It's amazing," I said, surveying the crowd proudly. "I don't think it could get much better than this."

But then Cleo grinned and said, "It just did. Check it out." She nodded to the crowd, and I turned to see Mei and Ben taking up a place in line with Leo and Ann. My heart skipped a beat. *Mei had come.*

Mei caught my eye. I noticed Ben give her a slight nudge, and she reluctantly made her way over to me.

"Hey," she said, avoiding my gaze. "This is quite a crowd."

"Yeah," I said nervously. "So . . . why are you here? I didn't think you'd come."

"I didn't think I would, either," she said quietly. "But Ben made me. He said if I kept moping around missing you, he was going to give all my pink clothes to Goodwill when I wasn't looking. I didn't really think he'd do it but, you know, just to be on the safe side . . ." She gave me a sheepish smile.

I giggled in spite of myself. After a second, Mei did, too. And suddenly the ice we'd been treading on gave in to our relieved laughter.

"I'm so sorry!" Mei cried, grabbing me in hug. "You were completely right to be mad at me for what happened at the concert. I shouldn't have left you alone in the theater, even if it *was* for my first kiss. I guess I went a little Ben crazy."

Just hearing her apology made me feel a thousand times better. Then I registered what else she'd said. "First kiss, huh?" I elbowed her. "It must've been pretty good to make you forget about me."

Mei blushed, then shook her head with a smile. "Seriously, I am sorry, Tessa. It's been sort of hard, figuring out how to balance a boyfriend and the rest of my life. But I think I'm learning."

I remembered how Mom and I had fought about the notion of balance, and my chest tightened. "Balance *is* hard," I told Mei. "And I'm sorry I was so tough on you about it. I guess I was a little . . ." I didn't want to cop to the word *jealous*, but I could see that Mei understood.

She grabbed my hand, nodding. "I never wanted to make you feel left out, or hurt. And I'm sorry that I was mean about the Great Pillow Fight, too. I shouldn't have called it stupid."

"It's okay," I said, squeezing her hand. "I'm sorry I got mad about you wanting to go to the dance. I should've tried to be more understanding. You just caught me off guard with everything. I mean, I never knew you hated the pillow fight so much."

"I don't hate it. It's just not my favorite thing to do." She paused, as if she was thinking carefully about how to say what came next. "You know, we have different interests, Tessa, but that's okay. We don't have to like all the same things, or even do all the same things, to stay best friends, right?"

I nodded, feeling hopeful. "So . . . we're still best friends?"

"Of course," Mei said, squeezing my hand back. "If you're cool with that?"

I laughed. "Very cool."

"Good, because I always wanted to be friends with a celebrity," Mei said, "and I think your fifteen minutes of fame just arrived. Look." She pointed toward the street, where a Channel Seven news truck was pulling up to the curb.

"Omigod," I whispered as Bev Channing and an onslaught of camera crew climbed out of the truck.

The camera crew set up in front of the Tasty Truck, and Bev walked over to me and Mei, already wearing her broadcasting smile. She introduced herself smoothly, then said, "Can you point me to the person in charge of this rally?"

I stammered an incoherent "U-um . . ." But then Gabe piped up from inside the truck.

"You're looking at her," he called, gesturing to me. "Her name is Tessa Kostas, and this was all her idea."

"Brilliant," said Bev. "Do you mind if I ask you a few questions?"

"U-uh," I stammered, then looked at Cleo, Gabe, and Mei,

who were all nodding more enthusiastically than a slew of bob-blehead dolls. "Sure."

The next thing I knew, I was being interviewed for the five o'clock evening news. Not the local news, either. The honest-to-goodness *national* news. The Tasty Truck's fight for Flavorfest was going to be broadcast across America. If that wasn't enough to get back Flavorfest, I didn't know what was.

By the time the news truck left, we were out of BLTs and the crowd was starting to slowly thin. But everyone was leaving with smiles on their faces and words of encouragement on their lips.

"You just wait," Mrs. Osaka said confidently as she gave me a parting hug. "We sent a message to Mr. Morgan that he can't possibly ignore."

"I hope so," I said.

Mei and Ben stuck around to help Cleo, Gabe, and me clean up and close down the truck.

"It's almost five o'clock," Cleo said when we finished. "I vote we head home, order pizza, and watch the Channel Seven evening news. Who's with me?"

I grinned at the unanimous "Yes!" While Gabe and Cleo parked the truck, I walked home with Mei and Ben. But when we stepped through our front door, I froze. My mouth fell open at the sight of Mom and Dad sitting on the sofa, waiting for me.

Mom's eyes met mine, her face expressionless.

"So," she said evenly. "How was the rally?"

# chapter
## twelve

I tiptoed inside, afraid that Mom would unleash a tirade about the evils of lying to parents and getting carried away with foolish dream-chasing. But she didn't.

Instead, she calmly and pleasantly offered everyone drinks and — shocker — homemade bacon-peanut-butter cookies.

"Bacon lovers' bliss!" Ben said around mouthfuls. "Tessa, did you make these?"

"No," I sputtered, confused. Where had they come from? It couldn't be . . .

I glanced at Mom in shock.

"Actually, *I* made them," Mom said, giving me a triumphant grin. "With a little help from your dad."

"She's actually not a bad cook," Dad said, "especially when you hold her cell phone hostage." Dad looked at me soberly. "But *you* were very busy today, too, weren't you?"

I sank down on the couch. "How'd you find out?"

"Oh, a reliable source did some reconnaissance this afternoon." He nodded toward Mom, who was passing Mei a cookie. "She got in from New York and decided she wanted to go say hi to you at the truck. The rest is history."

Just then, Gabe and Cleo walked in the door, and they both stopped cold. "So, I'm guessing we've been outed?" Cleo asked me.

"But I think we're forgiven," I said hopefully, and Dad nodded in confirmation.

"Then what are we waiting for?" Gabe cried, grabbing the TV remote. "It's five o'clock!"

Within seconds, Bev Channing's glamorous face had appeared on the screen.

"Today, we're taking a look at how an often-overlooked community of food truckers found their voice through one brave girl named Tessa Kostas."

Whoops and hollers exploded through the family room while I shushed everyone in embarrassment.

"Tessa," Bev continued, "tell us why you're fighting so hard to save Flavorfest."

I saw my face on-screen, a very odd sensation. I was surprised to see that my overalls didn't look half bad.

"Flavorfest showcases the talents of some amazing chefs in our community," I watched myself say. "Food trucks don't have long lives like restaurants, and they have to fight to survive. Flavorfest is the one time of year they get to shine in the spotlight. And since they create such delicious food for people every day and everywhere in this city, don't they deserve it?"

Had I really been so articulate? I almost couldn't believe it myself, except I felt Dad patting my back with pride.

Bev nodded. "And what would you say to people who have concerns about the quality and safety of the food from these trucks?"

"I'd bet any one of them that we keep our truck cleaner than they keep their own kitchens, and we have the five-star health and safety ranking to prove it." I smiled at the camera. "And if they don't believe me, they can stop by our truck any time, any day, for a tour." I pointed toward the Tasty Truck, and the camera zoomed in on it.

Everyone burst into applause around me.

"Go, Tessa!" Cleo and Mei cheered, and I felt my cheeks warm at the attention. I didn't really care about being semifamous; I just wanted to know if our rally had been effective. I leaned forward so that I could hear the rest of the broadcast. Bev went on to interview other people in the crowd, including a lot of the food-truck owners.

"Of course we came to the rally today," said Mrs. Bisrati. "The Flavorfest award we got two years ago for our falafel is the reason why we're still in business today. We need Flavorfest, and this year is no different."

"Yes, restaurants help our community," said Mr. Hirschorn, the owner of the cupcake truck, "but so do food trucks. Flavorfest is one of the ways we celebrate that every year. If Flavorfest goes, will food trucks be next?"

Next, Mr. Morgan appeared on-screen in a jogging suit, looking disgruntled and disheveled, like he'd just been interrupted in the middle of a workout.

"It's obvious that a lot of effort went into the rally," he said, "and I commend these food truckers' persistence. But I'm sorry to say it hasn't changed anything. The Taste of San Fran festival will still be held on February eighth, as scheduled. Now, if you'll excuse me . . ." He put his hand in front of the lens, and the camera shot back to Bev.

I didn't hear the rest of the broadcast. My stomach had fallen to the floor. Someone clicked off the TV, and silence took over the room. I could feel everyone looking at me, waiting for me to say something. But I couldn't bring myself to look at anyone.

I stood up, keeping my eyes focused on the carpet. "I guess that's it, then." My voice was high-pitched, straining for a carefree tone. "Oh well. We tried."

The words were all wrong, too casual for the weight of the moment, but they were all I could say.

"You know, all that chanting at the rally today kind of gave me a headache," I continued. "I'm just going to hang in my room for a while." I managed a shaky smile, waving to Mei and Ben. "I'll see you guys at school on Monday."

I was safe behind the closed door of my room before the first tear fell, but once it did, I couldn't stop the flood. I wasn't usually much of a crier, but when I did cry, it was the gushing, hiccupping, last-for-an-hour kind of torrent. It wasn't the kind of cry you wanted people to witness, so when I heard the first knock on my door, I didn't answer.

"Tessa, it's me." Mei's voice came through muffled from the other side of the door. "Ben just went home. Do you want to talk?" A full minute passed before she gave up. "Okay. Well, call me when you feel up to it. I'm sending you telepathic hugs. Bye."

Even through my tears, that made me smile.

I was planning to ignore the second knock, too, but then I heard, "Honey? It's Mom. Please let me in."

I lifted my head off the pillow. Normally, I wouldn't have let her in, either. But . . . today she'd baked bacon-peanut-butter cookies . . . from scratch. Clearly this wasn't an ordinary day for ordinary behavior. So I opened the door for her.

She took one look at my streaming eyes, and pulled me into her arms. I couldn't remember the last time I'd been there, tucked beneath her chin like a preschooler. But it felt warm and homey and . . . perfect.

"I'm so sorry, honey," she whispered into my curls. "For everything."

Yeesh. Now I was crying even more.

"I tried so hard," I blubbered. "For once I wanted to fix a problem instead of making one. I know I can be forgetful and irresponsible. And I'm sorry, because I know you want me to be this person you think I should be. But I'm not like you and Dad. I don't like numbers and logical thinking. I mean, nobody wakes up in the morning craving a good, solid math problem. But then there's bacon." I sniffled forlornly. "Who doesn't crave bacon?"

Mom laughed, brushing my hair back from my face. "That's a good point."

"I know you hate that I love working at the Tasty Truck," I continued, letting all my frustrations spill out. "But I thought if I could get Flavorfest back on track and the Bacon Me Crazy BLT won the Flavorfest Best Award, then I could keep the Tasty Truck from having to shut down, and you'd finally think I was doing something that mattered."

Mom shook her head, looking crestfallen. "Tessa, I don't hate that you work at the truck. I love that you have a passion for cooking. It's not something I've ever enjoyed, but you're not me, and I don't want or expect you to *be* me. Finding a passion like that in life is rare and lucky." She kissed the top of my head. "I'm so proud of what you did today. Seeing you speaking so clearly and with so much conviction on TV just now . . . I was blown away. I saw a spark in you that I'd never seen before, maybe because I was working too much. I don't know. But I could scarcely believe that such a strong-minded, fervent young woman could be my daughter."

I stared at her, shocked that this was actually Mom talking.

"I'm sorry if I haven't come across as supportive of your job at the Tasty Truck," she went on. "I probably came down too hard on you at times. But the fact of the matter is . . ." She gave a short laugh. "I was jealous."

I gaped at her. "What?"

She nodded. "It's true. I was jealous that Cleo got to spend so much time with you while I was working. The two of you have so much in common, and you and I are . . ."

"Different?" I offered.

She laughed. "To say the least. The point is, when you and Cleo got so close, I got . . . lonely." She rolled her eyes. "Oh, listen to me. That probably doesn't make any sense. . . ."

"No," I said. "No, it does." It made perfect sense. If there was one thing I'd gotten a good handle on lately, it was that lonely feeling that comes when someone you care about forgets about you. "I'm sorry. I didn't know."

"Don't be," Mom said. "I wouldn't even have told you now, except I thought I should, because things are about to change."

My eyes welled again. "You mean I won't be able to work at the Tasty Truck anymore?"

Mom smiled. "No. I mean that *I'm* not going to be working so much anymore. Your dad and I have been talking about it. I'm going to cut back on my work hours a little bit. I told my boss that this trip to New York would have to be my last business trip for a while, and she okayed that. This way, I'll be around more often to help you with your homework."

"Or maybe with cooking?" I said hopefully.

She laughed, hugging me. "If you can be patient with me."

"I will be. Thanks, Mom." I hadn't realized how much I'd longed for more of Mom's free time, until she offered it to me. But once she did, a welcoming warmth swept through me.

"So . . ." She peered down into my face. "I'm sure you're still upset about Flavorfest, but are you feeling any better at all? I know I'm sort of a rookie with these mother/daughter talks, but I'm trying."

I smiled, then kissed her cheek. "I do feel better. Much better."

"Oh, good." Mom looked grateful and relieved. Then she straightened and stood up. "I think I'll go make another batch of those cookies. Want to help?"

I didn't, not when I was sure it would only remind me of all the amazing recipes we weren't going to be able to take to

Flavorfest. But I also didn't want to disappoint Mom when things were improving between us. So I pushed Flavorfest to the back of my mind.

"Sure, Mom," I said. "But I'll have to keep a close eye on you. You know you can't use the oven without proper supervision."

Mom laughed. "Of course."

"We'll start with the basics," I said, leading the way into the kitchen. I reached into the drawer closest to the stove. "These . . . are called measuring spoons."

Mom rolled her eyes. "I can tell you're going to enjoy this."

I grinned. "You have no idea."

Sunday morning, I decided to introduce Mom to Cleo's roof garden. We were crouched over the fragrant herb beds, enjoying the feel of the sun on our backs, when the roof-access door opened.

I glanced up in time to see Asher step onto the roof. A baseball cap shaded his handsome face and his arms were crossed over his green T-shirt.

Just the sight of him sent my nerves reeling. My trowel slipped out of my hand, clattering to the gravel.

"I'll get it," Asher said, already reaching down.

"And . . . I'll go downstairs and get us some hot chocolate," Mom said, taking a cue from my flustered face. "Be back in a bit."

She disappeared through the door. The instant she was gone, I blurted, "Asher, I'm so sorry about everything I said to you. I know what you did for us with Karrie and the brownies, and I . . ." I swallowed and tried to talk over the noise of my hammering heart. "I want to thank you . . . so much."

"You're welcome," Asher said, ducking his head with a small smile. "I should've been honest with you about Mr. Morgan. But I was afraid you'd freak out if you knew, and then . . ."

"I *did* freak out." I gave a short laugh. "But I completely overreacted. Everything was falling apart all at once, and I was just so stressed, and . . ." I bit my lip. "And I really wanted you to be at the rally. I thought . . . I guess I thought we were becoming good friends."

"We were," Asher said. "We still are, I hope." A question came into his eyes. "If *you* want to be."

My heart raced. "I do."

"I wanted to be at the rally," Asher said. "I thought about you — I mean, the rally — all day long." His cheeks took on a reddish tinge and my stomach flipped. "But I still knew I couldn't go." He looked at me intently. "I know you think I don't stand up enough for what I believe in, and maybe you're right. I'm trying to be better about that, telling people what I really think, no matter what. That's part of why I called Karrie on her lie. But this was different. This was something I had to do for Mom. So, if you're going to stay mad at me, then —"

"No," I interrupted. "I understand why you couldn't come. It's okay." I sighed. "Besides, the rally didn't change anything anyway. Flavorfest is canceled."

"But maybe it doesn't have to be," Asher said mysteriously. "That's the other reason I'm here."

"What do you mean?" I felt a stirring of hopefulness.

"I found out something about Mr. Morgan yesterday," Asher said, an impish glint lighting up his eyes. "Something that might give you one last chance to win him over. It's a long shot, though, and it's not really something I'd be able to help with."

I'd take a long shot. At this point, I'd take anything. I nodded at Asher with a smile. "So . . . tell me!"

By the time Mom returned with three steaming cups of hot cocoa, Asher and I had a plan in place. The chances of it working were slim, but we didn't have anything to lose. There was only one problem with our plan: getting it past my mom.

As she handed me a cup brimming with marshmallows, I took a deep breath and jumped right in.

"Mom," I said. "Asher thinks he knows a way that we still might be able to save Flavorfest."

"Really?" Mom said enthusiastically. "That would be so wonderful."

Asher nodded. "But, Mrs. Kostas, it's a little complicated."

Mom looked at me, and I forced myself to say the words.

"I'd have to miss a few hours of school tomorrow," I said in a rush.

There. I'd said it. But I knew it was a lost cause. Never in a million years would Mom agree to pull me out of school for something like this. In her eyes, it would probably be just as bad as ditching. But then she surprised me. Instead of an instantaneous *no*, as I'd feared, she said, "So, what's the plan?"

Mom didn't say a word as Asher explained everything, but she didn't grimace or frown or laugh, either. Finally, when Asher had finished, we waited for her answer.

I held my breath while Mom studied her hot cocoa mug intensely. When she finally looked up, it was with a mischievous grin I'd never seen on her face before.

"Well, Tessa," she said, "it looks like you and I are both going to come home sick tomorrow."

I grinned at her and Asher, barely believing my good luck. "Oh yes," I said, putting a hand to my forehead. "I think I feel a case of the hookies coming on. It should hit me, say, around eleven?"

Mom nodded. "I'll be outside the school. Eleven sharp."

# chapter
# thirteen

At exactly a quarter to eleven on Monday, I caught a full-blown case of the hookies, complete with nausea, headache, and lethargy. The school nurse said I didn't have a fever, but since this was my first visit to the nurse's office ever, she decided I must really be sick.

Ten minutes later, I was headed down the hallway to grab my books, very pleased with the way my "illness" had played out. I opened my locker, and when I did, a note fluttered to my feet. I picked it up and read:

*Good luck today. I can't wait to hear how it goes. Fingers crossed. Ash*

I smiled, tucked the note into my jeans pocket, then hurried outside to the curb, where Mom was waiting.

"Did you get everything?" I asked Mom as I climbed into the car.

Mom nodded to the backseat. There were delivery bags full of the BLTs Cleo and I had made last night, our bacon-bits brownies, and our bacon-peanut-butter cookies.

"Operation Bacon Bust is underway," Mom said. She hit the gas, and my heartbeat accelerated right along with it.

After wading through midday traffic in the financial district, we finally pulled up in front of 555 California Street. It was the second-tallest building in all of San Francisco, and headquarters to Morgan Food Enterprises.

I grabbed the delivery bags out of the backseat, feeling slightly nauseous for real this time.

Mom blew me a kiss. "I'm going to find a parking garage, but

I'll meet you right outside the building when you're finished. Good luck."

"Thanks." I shut the door, gulped in air, and started walking.

Through the gleaming glass doors of the building, there was a sleek marble security desk with an intimidating-looking security guard behind it.

"Lunch delivery for Mr. Morgan," I said, giving the guard an über-friendly smile.

The guard's expression stayed as still as stone. "One moment, please," he said, picking up the phone. After a series of low grunts, he finally nodded to the elevators. "Fiftieth floor."

I hurried to the elevators, afraid that at any second he'd recognize me as an imposter and yell for me to stop. But the elevator shot upward, and a minute later, I was walking up to Mr. Morgan's receptionist, who was blessedly busy on the phone. She glanced at my delivery bags impatiently, then pointed to a conference room at the end of the hallway.

My heartbeat was a booming cannon in my ears as I approached the glass-walled conference room. Then I saw him. Mr. Morgan was there, just as Asher had said he'd be, sitting with a dozen managers from the finest restaurants in San Francisco.

Asher had explained the whole thing to me yesterday. Asher had overheard Mr. Morgan telling his mom about a big lunch-time meeting he'd be having to plan the Taste of San Fran. Mr. Morgan mentioned having sandwiches brought in for everyone from Baughman's Bread, one of San Fran's poshest downtown cafés.

In an act that was about to be proven completely genius or utterly stupid, I'd called Baughman's last night and, posing as Mr. Morgan's assistant, canceled his entire lunch order.

Which meant that the Tasty Truck, and *not* Baughman's, would be filling the lunch order today for Mr. Morgan. Now the rest was up to me and the Bacon Me Crazy BLTs.

I tried to calm my racing heart as I swung open the conference-room door and stepped inside with my bags. Mr. Morgan looked up and frowned, and for one terrifying moment, I thought he recognized me from my twenty-second sound bite on the evening news. But then his eyes settled on my delivery bags.

"Oh yes," Mr. Morgan said. "Lunch. Thank you." He nodded toward the door. "My receptionist will pay you."

"You're welcome," I managed to say over my pounding pulse as I set the delivery bags on the table. I didn't care about getting paid. I just wanted the plan to work.

I walked *very slowly* toward the door as the men and women around the conference table unwrapped the sandwiches. I glanced over my shoulder as they all began taking bites out of their BLTs. One woman smiled, and I heard several "Mmmms." I got to the doorway just as Mr. Morgan took the first bite of his sandwich.

And that's where I stopped, unable to take another step until I saw his reaction.

He chewed for what seemed like forever, then closed his eyes. He was smiling. And then he said it.

"Mmmm."

His eyes flew open and instantly found mine. "Young lady, please come back!"

Now my heart was performing somersaults. "I-is something wrong?" I stuttered.

"This sandwich . . ." he mumbled around a second bite. "I've never had anything like it before from Baughman's. It's . . . it's fantastic!"

A mile-wide grin broke out on my face.

"Actually, the Bacon Me Crazy BLT didn't come from Baughman's," I said triumphantly. "It came from the Tasty Truck, the food truck that sits on the corner of Hyde and Lombard. It was nominated for the Flavorfest Best Award this year but, as you know, there won't be a Flavorfest." I sighed forlornly, drawing on the few things Mei had tried to teach me about stage acting. "Without the Flavorfest award, the Tasty Truck might not be around much longer, and neither will this BLT."

Mr. Morgan looked down at the sandwich as if he was witnessing some sort of great tragedy.

"Well, I have a lot more deliveries to make," I added breezily, giving him a friendly wave, "but there's a Tasty Truck menu in the bag. My advice is to get the BLT while you can, before it's gone forever."

And after giving him that food for thought, I walked away.

I didn't know what would happen now. That was entirely up to Mr. Morgan. Still, though, I couldn't help feeling a sense of victory as I hurried outside to Mom's waiting car.

Mom and I played legitimate hooky together for the rest of the afternoon, going out for frozen yogurt in Nob Hill and then making the trek on the Bart train to Vinyl to browse LPs. It turned out Mom was an even bigger Beatles fan than Cleo (shocker).

We had a great time and, miraculously, didn't fight once. Mom did have to shake me out of daydreaming a couple times, mostly because I kept thinking about the bliss on Mr. Morgan's face when he took his first bite of that BLT. I know a true bacon lover when I see one — the relish in their eyes as they catch the first scent of it sizzling, the smile sweeping across their face as they bite into a crisp strip fresh off the skillet. And I knew beyond a doubt that Mr. Morgan was a bacon lover.

But I still wasn't sure that would be enough to change anything.

Just before school got out for the day, Mom dropped me off outside the Bayview entrance so I could walk to the Tasty Truck with Mei and fill her in. The instant she came out of the school doors, we were back in our daily routine, as if our fight had never happened. Except it wasn't just the two of us anymore. Asher, Tristan, Ben, Leo, and Ann came with us, too, forming a posse of moral support around me. As we turned down Hyde Street, laughing and talking about my bait and switch with Mr. Morgan, I realized how much livelier and fun my after-school walk had suddenly become. When I'd started this semester, I'd been happy to have Mei as my only really close friend. But over the last few weeks, my circle of friends had grown, and now I couldn't imagine what it would be like without any of them.

When we were half a block away from the Tasty Truck, Asher nudged me and pointed ahead. "Guess who came back for a second helping?"

I looked up to see Mr. Morgan standing at the Tasty Truck, chatting happily away with Cleo as he finished off another BLT.

"He's brave to show his face at the truck," Tristan said. "I'm surprised Cleo's actually feeding him."

"Maybe he comes in peace," I said hopefully.

"Do you think that's possible for the Grinch Who Stole Flavorfest?" Mei asked.

"Watch it," Asher said half teasingly. "That may be my future stepdad you're talking about."

There were groans and laughs, and Ben said, "Just what you need, *another* penthouse."

Then everyone was laughing, even Asher. But the laughter died down as we got to the truck, and Mr. Morgan came toward me.

"Ah, the person I was looking for," he said, extending his hand. "The savvy business girl after my own heart."

I shook his hand firmly. I hoped I could pull off a no-nonsense business-girl look while my knees were knocking.

"Your aunt just gave me a tour of your Tasty Truck, and I have to admit, I'm impressed. It was spotlessly clean both inside and out. Even some of my own restaurant kitchens could take a lesson from that truck."

"Thanks," I said nervously.

He nodded. "But I'm even more impressed with the bravado of your little sandwich change-up at my office earlier," he said. "At first, I couldn't figure out how you timed your performance so perfectly with my schedule. But now . . ." He wagged a scolding finger jokingly at Asher. "I know."

Asher met Mr. Morgan's eyes squarely. "We just wanted to give you a taste of what you might be missing if Flavorfest gets canceled."

"And," I added, "to prove to you that food trucks can make food as delicious as any restaurant can."

Mr. Morgan nodded. "Well, it worked." He straightened the lapels of his suit, as if he was prepping for a speech. "You don't have to worry about Flavorfest anymore. It would be a down-right sin to let that BLT lose its chance at the Flavorfest Best Award. So, I'm going to postpone the Taste of San Fran festival until next fall." He smiled. "Flavorfest is back on for this Saturday!"

A deafening cheer exploded from all of us, and everyone was high-fiving and dancing on the sidewalk. In my delirious joy, I grabbed the closest person in a fierce hug, then pulled away, flustered, when I realized it was Asher.

"S-sorry," I stammered, my cheeks burning.

But Asher grinned. "Don't be," he said, looking pleased instead of embarrassed. I could feel someone else watching our exchange unfold, and when I glanced up, I saw it was Tristan. He was wearing a thoughtful, almost serious expression.

Asher must've seen it, too, because he instantly stepped away from me self-consciously. Tristan dropped his eyes. I studied Asher and Tristan, trying to figure out what had just happened. Did Asher think Tristan liked me? Was he afraid of making Tristan jealous? I didn't have any time to figure it out, because Mr. Morgan was clearing his throat and checking his cell phone.

"I have some important meetings to get to," he said now, "but I'm planning on being at Flavorfest next Saturday, and I expect the BLT to win." He gave me a mock-serious look. "Don't disappoint me."

I smiled. "I'll do my best."

"See you later, Asher," Mr. Morgan said to Asher a little stiffly. But there was something sweet about it, as if Mr. Morgan was nervous about Asher liking him. Maybe he wasn't the worst guy in the world after all.

Asher said bye to Mr. Morgan. He started to walk away, then turned back to Cleo and Gabe.

"You know," Mr. Morgan said. "I'll take one more BLT for the road."

After he left, I let out an earsplitting whoop and Cleo leaned out the window to give me a high five. "We did it!" I cried.

"*You* did it," she said, grinning. "But, oh my god, do we have work to do now! We've got to get the word out to the other trucks that Flavorfest is back on. And now we only have five days to prep, and we're not even close to ready."

"I'll send out an e-mail blast to the other trucks right now," Gabe said, his fingers already flying over his phone screen. "And we need to decide on our menu. . . ."

"About our menu," I started. "Should we make it all bacon-themed for Flavorfest? I mean, it's what everyone loves the most about our truck. And all the other food trucks in town have their specialties, like Signor Antonio's gelato, and the Bisratis' falafels. Why can't our specialty be bacon? Bacon on everything, all the time?"

"I'm totally into that," Tristan piped up. "I'd eat my way through every single thing on the menu." Ben nodded enthusiastically.

Cleo and Gabe looked at each other, and wide grins broke out on both their faces.

"A theme menu is a great idea," Gabe said.

"We can try it at Flavorfest," Cleo said excitedly, "and if the menu gets a good response, then we can keep it permanently. But that means we have even more to do to get ready."

"So what are we waiting for?" Asher said. "Let's get to work."

"Wow," I said, staring at him in mock shock. "I never thought I'd hear you say those words."

"You finally corrupted me," he said teasingly. "I'm ruined for life."

"Glad to hear it," I replied with a grin. "But before we start, there's something I need to do first."

I pulled out my cell phone, and she picked up on the first ring.

"Mom?" I smiled into the phone. "You're not going to believe what happened. . . ."

For the next few days, Cleo, Gabe, and I worked frantically to get the truck's menu ready for Flavorfest. Our kitchen became bacon central. We tried over a dozen different bacon-themed sandwich and dessert recipes. By Friday, we were exhausted, but it was the satisfying kind of exhaustion that comes from working hard at something you love. Our menu was a masterpiece of bacon cuisine, and I thought we were prepared for anything and everything.

But I wasn't prepared for what happened after school on Friday afternoon. When Asher and I got to the Tasty Truck, Gabe met us at the back door, his face tight with worry. Gabe was usually so laid back. Just seeing him like this filled me with sudden dread.

"What's wrong?" I asked.

"It's Cleo," Gabe started. "She wasn't feeling good this morning. . . ."

"I know," I said, my pulse quickening. "She said she didn't want any breakfast because her stomach was bothering her."

Gabe nodded. "Well, it got worse, so your mom took her to the ER."

I gasped. "The hospital? Why?"

"It's appendicitis." Gabe's voice quavered. "Your mom just called a few minutes ago to tell me."

"Omigod," I whispered, a cold clamminess shooting through me. "Will she be okay?"

Gabe nodded, checking his watch. "She's going into surgery right now, and I have to get over to the hospital. I was hoping you guys could close up the truck for me? Your dad's on his way, too, and he can park it after you're finished."

"Okay," Asher said before I could manage to get the words out through the thick clouds of worry in my head.

"There's something else, too." Gabe sighed. "We're completely out of Cleo's special sauce. I'm at a total loss. I don't have the first clue how to make it, and I can't exactly ask Cleo now that she's about to be operated on. I'll probably be at the hospital all night, so I don't even have time to *try* to make the sauce. And there's no way we can pull off Flavorfest without it."

"Doesn't Cleo have a recipe for it?" Asher asked, glancing from me to Gabe.

"She's never written one down," I said. "She keeps it all up here," I added, pointing to my head.

Gabe paused, seeming to think things over. "Maybe it would be better if we just dropped out."

"No!" I cried, so loudly that Gabe and Asher both stared at me. "We are *not* dropping out," I continued, my heart racing. "We can't do that to Cleo. The Tasty Truck needs Flavorfest too much." I started pacing the length of the truck, feeling my worry transforming into fierce determination. "I'm going to fix this."

Asher raised a skeptical eyebrow. "How, exactly?"

"*I'm* going to make the special sauce," I said staunchly. "I'll re-create the recipe." Gabe and Asher shook their heads, but when I glared at them, they froze. "I can do it. I've watched her making it before, and I remember most of the ingredients she used. I just have to get the combo right. . . ."

"I don't know," Gabe said. "The judges will know if it tastes wrong. . . ."

"It won't taste wrong," I said adamantly. "It'll be perfect, and we'll have it in time for tomorrow. We'll close up the truck, and then I'll start working on the recipe."

"I'll help," Asher volunteered. I glanced at him in surprise, and he smiled. "Well, I'm not about to let you crash and burn alone."

"Thanks, I think," I said with a laugh, and a sense of relief. "And we are *not* crashing and burning." Then I turned to Gabe. "So?"

The silence dragged on as I stared at him, waiting. Then, finally, Gabe gave a reluctant nod. "Okay," he said. "Give it a shot, and we'll see what happens. But if the sauce isn't perfect, we put the kibosh on Flavorfest. Deal?"

"Deal."

Gabe grabbed his keys and headed for the door. "I'll call as soon as I have news!" he yelled over his shoulder as he stepped off the curb to hail a cab.

"Tell Cleo I love her!" I called to him.

I took a deep breath, my fear and worry for Cleo threatening to turn me into a quivering wreck. But instead of giving in to it, I pushed it away and squared my shoulders. The best thing I could do for Cleo right now was find a way to make her sauce.

"I'm sorry about Cleo," Asher said, his brow furrowed with concern. "Are you okay?"

"I have to be," I said firmly. Cleo had always been the one person in my family who had faith in me. There was no way I could let her down now. Not when, for the first time ever, she needed my help more than I needed hers.

"So," Asher said, glancing dubiously at the small city of spices and condiments on my kitchen counter, "what do we do now?"

"We blend," I said. Even my worry and stress couldn't keep the grin from my face as I put on my apron and grabbed my mixing bowl. This was my absolute favorite thing about cooking. Starting with the great unknown, then tossing dashes and sprinkles of spices haphazardly in a bowl until you slowly winnow them down into the perfect combination of flavors.

Asher picked up his own bowl hesitantly. "Um, aren't you going to tell me what to start with?"

"Nope," I said. "That's the best part. It's trial and error. A combination might be brilliant, or completely putrid. You just have to mix, then taste."

"But don't you at least know some of what goes into the sauce?" Asher asked. "You said you'd seen Cleo make it before."

"Um, I might have exaggerated slightly when I said I knew what Cleo put in the sauce." Asher's frown deepened, and I tossed my hands up helplessly. "I couldn't just tell Gabe that I didn't know what I was doing. He would've given up! Now at least we have a chance."

"But what are you going to do if you can't figure out the recipe?" Asher asked.

I wagged a scolding finger at him. "No way. No defeatist attitude for me. I will not be conquered by a tablespoon-sized mystery. I *will* uncover the secret of the sauce."

Asher's frown caved into laughter, and he shook his head. "Okay, Dr. Frankensauce, whatever you say. Let's blend away."

I smiled enthusiastically, and together, we bent over our mixing bowls. The first combination I tried, one with mayonnaise and red wine vinegar, curdled. And Asher didn't fare much better. He tried combining chipotle with pickle relish, which sounded good until I smelled it.

"I see you gagging, you know," Asher said, eyeing me suspiciously as I tucked my nose into the crook of my arm. "It's not *that* bad."

"Nooooo," I said, "not bad at all. It only smells like a dead skunk."

He sniffed it, then made a concerted effort not to wince. "*I* think it smells like roses." Then we both burst out laughing. It felt good to have fun with Asher again, and I promised myself that even if he did end up going to the dance with Karrie, I would try not to let it affect our friendship.

But three hours later, our laughter was harder to come by. We were each on our tenth version of the sauce, and I was pretty sure that, at this point, my taste buds were going completely numb. My smile was waning, and the tablespoon-sized mystery was winning.

I dipped a spoon into the bowl containing the latest batch and brought it slowly to my lips. There were the same flavors I recognized from the previous tries: a hint of mayonnaise and chipotle, the creamy goodness of avocado, with the undertones of lemon juice and Dijon mustard. It should've been right. But it wasn't.

I tossed the spoon into the sink, where it clattered into the pile of others. "It's not right!" I slumped over the kitchen counter, a suffocating panic starting to rise in me. "Wait. We haven't tried fresh dill yet. Maybe that will work." I grabbed a bunch off the counter, then hurriedly reached into a drawer, slamming it shut before I realized my finger was still inside. A yowl of pain ripped out of me, and then I was jumping around the kitchen, clutching my fingernail and whimpering.

Asher's eyes glinted, but when I hissed, "Don't you dare laugh," he took the threat in my voice seriously.

"Let me see," he said, and before I could protest, he'd taken my hand into his own and begun rubbing my finger soothingly. Lightning zinged through me at the warmth of his touch. I found myself thinking that he could hold my hand, just like that, forever. But all too soon, he slid my hand out of his, giving it a friendly pat. "Better?"

It took me a few seconds to find my voice. "Um . . . yeah. Thanks."

He shook his head. "Maybe you should let me do the chopping. I'm not sure you can be trusted with a knife."

"Ha," I said, then added seriously, "We're running out of time." I sighed. "I'm starting to think we're never going to get it right."

Asher started pulling the herbs out of my basket, then stopped. "Maybe we're not getting it right because we're going about it the wrong way."

"What do you mean?"

"We've been making the sauce, then tasting it. Maybe we need to taste it first."

"Huh?" I stared at him.

"Describe the way Cleo's sauce tasted . . . down to every last detail."

I looked at him uncertainly, then took a deep breath, searching my memory. "It tastes cool and tangy, like summertime barbecues, but also like a sleepy Sunday breakfast. It tastes of

avocado and lemon, mayonnaise and mustard. But . . . wait!"
My mouth started to water. "There's something else . . .
something smoky and nutty and crisp."

*Smoky and crisp . . .*

We grinned at each other as the realization hit us at the
same time.

"Bacon!" we cried.

I slapped a hand to my head and one of my bobby pins sprang
loose. "I can't believe it took me this long to figure it out! Cleo
uses crushed bacon *in* the special sauce!"

"I knew you'd get it eventually." Asher laughed as I performed
a happy dance around the counter.

But I didn't let myself celebrate for long. "Come on," I said,
grabbing some bacon out of the fridge and tossing it to him.
"Fire up the stove. Let's see if we're right."

Asher saluted me. "Bacon detail. I'm on it."

We went to work, using all the same ingredients we'd used in
the last batch of sauce, but this time, adding in a sprinkling of
crushed bacon. When we'd made enough sauce to sample, I tried
tasting it again.

"Mmmm," I said. "It's perfect! Just like Cleo's."

Asher agreed, taking another big bite. "It's like a 'Hallelujah' chorus in my mouth."

After that, it didn't take much longer to make a batch big enough for Flavorfest. When we were finished, we carried the containers of sauce to the fridge triumphantly, then collapsed onto the stools at the counter, exhausted but jubilant.

Then the phone rang, making us both jump.

I saw Mom's cell on the caller ID, and my stomach lurched. "Mom?" I answered anxiously.

"Cleo's fine," she said. "She's awake, and Gabe was with her when I left the hospital a little while ago."

I let go of the breath I'd been holding. "What a relief." I grinned at Asher, giving him a thumbs-up. When I got off the phone, the leaden weight on my chest had lifted.

"Gabe and my dad are staying at the hospital for a while," I said to Asher, "but my mom will be here soon. She can drive you home."

We finished cleaning up the kitchen, and by the time Mom pulled up outside, we had everything laid out and ready for the big day tomorrow.

We were making our way to the door when Asher stopped to pick something up off the floor. "Here's that bobby pin you lost before," he said. "What was this one for?"

"A reminder to say thank you," I said. "For all your help today."

He smiled. "You're welcome." He slid the bobby pin back into my curls and his fingers inadvertently brushed against my cheek, electrifying my skin. Then he jerked his hand back awkwardly.

"So, I'll see you tomorrow at Flavorfest," he said as I walked him to the door.

"Tomorrow," I answered when I finally found my voice. The door shut, and I collapsed onto my stool, pressing my hot forehead against the cool countertop. So much for taking our friendship in stride. I knew Asher would never like me the way I hoped he would. But I, on the other hand, was an absolute goner.

# chapter
# fourteen

"We need another five BLTs, stat," Gabe said from where he was seated on his stool manning the orders at the window. "One with extra sauce."

"We're on it," I said, piling piping-hot bacon strips onto the toasted bread. "Mom, can you —"

"Tomatoes," she said before I could even finish. "Coming right up."

I glanced at Mom, and she caught my eye and smiled. We'd been working nonstop since the second the Flavorfest gates had opened at ten A.M. sharp, and there was no sign of the crowds or our orders letting up. Maybe it was the fact that the community had fought so hard for Flavorfest this year, or maybe it was the Channel Seven news broadcast that had done it. Whatever the reason, the number of people attending Flavorfest today was record-breaking. I'd heard Bev Channing say so herself when she came by our truck a little while ago.

All of our food-truck friends were here with their spruced-up trucks. When I looked out the window of our truck, it was onto a shiny fleet of multicolored trucks as far as the eye could see. Streamers and balloons hung from almost every window, and happy, hungry fair-goers wandered around, enjoying the sunshine and the live music playing from the stage by the judges' booth. And everyone, of course, was eating as much of the delicious smorgasbord as their stomachs could handle.

Mom, who'd never been to Flavorfest before, was totally impressed.

"I had no idea it was this big," she kept saying.

Seeing her in an apron, working in the Tasty Truck, still threw me for a loop, but it was a welcome sight. Because Cleo was still in the hospital, Mom had volunteered to help Gabe and me. It might've been easier to have Asher help, but he was working the Flavorfest crowd, handing out VOTE FOR THE BACON ME CRAZY BLT buttons to anyone who would take them.

Besides, Mom had asked to help so eagerly that I knew she was looking at this as a mother/daughter bonding opportunity. And we were having a lot of fun so far.

"How am I doing?" she asked uncertainly, handing me the freshly sliced tomatoes.

"Great," I said. "Do you need a break?"

"Are you kidding?" Mom said. "Look at that line out there. And the judges haven't even come by yet. There's no way I'm taking a break!"

I laughed. "I'm glad I finally found a good use for your workaholic side."

Mom raised an eyebrow. "Very funny."

I handed Gabe our fresh batch of BLTs, and he suddenly nudged me and whispered, "They're here."

I looked out the window. Two men and one woman wearing official FLAVORFEST JUDGE badges were rapidly approaching the truck. I sucked in a breath as my pulse began pounding.

"We'll take three of your Bacon Me Crazy BLTs," the woman said, her eyes scanning the menu soberly. "And one bacon-bits brownie, one bacon-peanut-butter cookie, and one strip of chocolate-covered bacon."

Gabe nodded, and Mom and I got right to work. I took special care to make each BLT, all the while thinking, *This is the one, the Flavorfest Best Award winner.* When everything was ready, we passed the goodies through the window, saying our thanks.

"Your bacon-themed menu . . ." one of the men said. "It's very clever. No one will walk away forgetting your bacon today, that's for sure." He held up the sandwich with a nod. "Thank you, and good luck."

Then, the three of them were gone, wading through the crowds.

"They're not going to eat them right now?" I cried in dismay.

Gabe laughed. "Patience, patience. They'll take them back to their booth so they can make notes while they eat."

"Notes?" I rolled my eyes. "That just takes all the fun out of it. Eating the BLT is supposed to be about your senses falling in love. The sauce zinging through your taste buds, the bacon popping and crackling between your teeth, the lettuce snapping . . ."

"They'll fall in love . . . *while* they're taking notes." Mom smiled and squeezed my hand. "Give them a chance, Tessa. Just try to stay calm. . . ."

Mom was good at calm; so was Gabe. *I* was not. The next three hours felt like the longest of my life. But finally, a loudspeaker crackled to life, announcing that the results from the judges' panel were in and that the votes from the crowd had been tallied. To win the award for Flavorfest Best, you had to have at least three out of four total votes. Each of the judges had one vote, and the crowd's votes, when they were tallied, counted as the fourth overall vote.

"Please have at least one representative from your truck on stage for the Flavorfest award announcement in five minutes."

The loudspeaker snapped off, and I looked at Gabe. "Are you ready?"

Gabe nodded, then grabbed his smartphone. "Wait a sec. Cleo's coming, too." He dialed her cell on Skype. Within seconds, Cleo's face appeared, tired but smiling, on Gabe's screen.

"Cleo!" I said. "I'm so glad you're okay."

"Hey," she said, waving from her hospital bed. "I heard what you did while I was in surgery yesterday, Tessa. Thanks for saving the day with the special sauce."

"It's not saved yet," I said nervously. "But we'll know in about ten minutes."

Cleo held up crossed fingers. "I'll be watching."

"And I'll be waiting to hear the news," Mom said. She'd be holding down the fort in the truck while Gabe and I braved the stage. She gave me a tight hug. "I'm so proud of you. Now, get out there and bring home the bacon."

I rolled my eyes, then laughed. "I'll try."

As Gabe and I began weaving through the crowd toward the stage, my laughter faded into nervousness. My legs started shaking so badly, I wasn't sure how I'd climb the steps up to the stage.

But that's when I saw Asher standing at the base of the stairs. His reassuring smile swept my breath away, but it also bolstered my courage.

"Go on," Gabe said, giving me a gentle shove forward. "He's waiting."

"B-but, what about you?" I stammered.

Gabe shook his head. "It's you and Asher now. Cleo's orders."

"That's right," Cleo piped up from Gabe's phone. "So get up there."

I took a deep breath, then walked toward Asher.

"I'm not sure I can do this," I whispered to him.

"Hey, you taught me how to cook," Asher said. "This should be a piece of cake compared to that, right?"

"You may be right," I said, and I felt some of my nervousness dissipate as I smiled. Together, Asher and I climbed the stairs and took our place in front of hundreds of cheering and applauding onlookers.

"Go, Tessa!" a chorus of voices hollered out from the crowd. I craned my neck, spotting Tristan, Ben, and Mei standing next to Gabe and waving. And, shockingly, there stood Mr. Morgan, with his arm around Asher's mom.

Somehow, seeing all of the encouraging faces — even Mr. Morgan's — gave me an extra boost of confidence. I waved back. No matter what happened in the next few minutes, I was proud that we'd come this far, and that I had such great friends by my side.

The woman judge I'd seen before took center stage and motioned for the crowd to quiet down.

"This had to be one of the closest competitions we've seen in years," she said into the microphone. "All of the nominees for the Flavorfest Best Award were exquisite, and I think I speak for all the judges when I say what a difficult decision we had to make." The other judges nodded, and the crowd rumbled their agreement.

"And now for the winners," she said. "Third place goes to the Gelatta Love truck for its *limoncello* gelato."

Asher and I burst into applause as Signor Antonio swept his fedora off and made a gallant bow. He took the third-place plaque and shouted, *"Grazie! Grazie!"* to the screaming crowd.

"Second place goes to the Chickpeas Please truck for its Famous Falafel," the judge announced, and Mrs. Bisrati graciously accepted the plaque while the crowd cheered.

"And now," the judge said, "for the first-place winner."

I swallowed, barely able to breathe or hear over the thundering of my heartbeat.

"This year's Flavorfest Best Award goes to . . . the Tasty Truck for the Bacon Me Crazy BLT with Tessa's special sauce!"

Applause and cheers exploded through the crowd. The judge turned toward Asher and me, expectantly holding out our plaque and waiting for one of us to step forward.

"Well, what are you waiting for?" Asher said, giving me a nudge. "Go up there and get our award."

But even through my daze of exhilaration, I hesitated. "But . . . she said *Tessa's* special sauce," I said.

"That's right," Asher said. "It was Cleo's idea to change the name on the entry. Gabe told me this morning. Cleo's sauce was great, but *yours* is even better." He pulled me into a hug that sent a shiver straight to my core. "You deserve this," he whispered. "Now . . . go!"

My head spun giddily. Then, scarcely believing it was actually me, I walked forward, beaming, to accept the award.

The second we stepped off the stage, Asher and I were surrounded. Mei got to me first, practically knocking me over with hugs, and then came Ben, Tristan, and Gabe, with Cleo blowing me mad kisses the whole time over Skype.

"We knew you'd win," Mei said. "But I wore my lucky skirt, just in case."

"Pink, of course," I said with a laugh.

"Of course," Mei said, grinning.

I glanced at Mr. Morgan, who was pulling Gabe aside.

"Have you and Cleo ever considered opening a franchise for the truck?" I heard Mr. Morgan saying. "I think there's great potential, and I own this amazing space that's vacant at the moment. . . ."

I glanced at Asher, and whispered, "Wow."

He grinned. "I guess there's an upside to my mom dating a restaurant tycoon."

"Hey, guys," Tristan said, "if I don't get my hands on one of the BLTs ASAP I'm going to get the shakes." Then he turned to everyone else. "I'm heading to the Tasty Truck. Who's coming?"

There was a resounding "yes," except for Asher, who said, "Tessa and I will meet you guys there in a minute."

My heart skittered as Tristan grinned at us, like he knew something delicious he wasn't about to share. Mei grinned, too, exchanging secretive looks with Ben. Obviously something big was going on, and I was the only one who didn't know what.

"See you in a few," Mei sang as she and Ben walked off.

And within seconds, Asher and I were alone on the outskirts of the slowly dispersing crowd.

"What's up with everybody?" I asked, feeling my temperature rising. "I figured they'd want to celebrate."

"They do," Asher said. "They're just waiting for me to get my act together."

"What do you mean?" I asked.

He took a deep breath and blew it out nervously. "See, there's this girl I've been meaning to ask to the Sweet Heart Ball," he said, "but I've kind of been a chicken about it."

My heart sank. "I know who you're talking about."

He stared at me, dumbfounded. "You do?"

I nodded. "And I know she'll say yes."

Asher smiled with relief. "You do?"

"Definitely," I said softly. "I mean, Karrie really likes you, and . . ." I couldn't find my voice anymore through my disappointment.

Asher blinked, then burst out laughing. "Tessa," he said, shaking his head in disbelief, "I'm not going to ask Karrie to the dance."

"You're . . . not?"

"No," he said quietly. "I know Karrie likes me, but I had a long talk with her this week, and now she knows that she and I will always be just friends. And she's okay with that, or, at least she will be when she's done tantruming." His eyes settled on mine, and I found myself getting lost in their deep amber color. "The girl I've been wanting to ask to the dance is, well, it's you."

*What?*

"Me?" I replied, dazed.

He nodded, his cheeks turning red. "Couldn't you tell?"

I shook my head, speechless. I'd thought that winning the Flavorfest award was a surreal moment — but that couldn't come close to this. Asher liked me? I was barely aware of the bustle of the crowd around me as Asher and I faced each other.

"I've liked you from that first day at the truck, when you called me conceited," Asher admitted, his blush deepening. He looked cuter by the minute. "Of course, I didn't realize it then. I think I really started to realize it that night of the concert, when we watched the meteor shower."

"Oh," I said softly, the memories washing over me. Had I been totally blind? Somehow I'd completely missed that while I'd been falling for Asher, he'd been falling for me, too.

"I wasn't sure how *you* felt, though," Asher went on, sounding nervous. "So I kind of sent Tristan to do some spy work for me, to try to maybe gauge what you were thinking."

"*Oh,*" I said again, only this time I finally understood why Tristan had been stopping by the truck and asking me so many questions. Especially about the dance. He'd been trying to figure out if I had a date yet or not, so that Asher could ask me. I made a mental note to thank him later.

"Wait." Asher's brow furrowed for a second. "Do *you* like Tristan?"

"No!" I said, still wrapping my head around the fact that I could make Asher Rivers jealous. "Not in that way. I mean, he's a great guy — nicer than I would've imagined a Beautiful Person could be —" I caught myself.

"Beautiful Person?" Asher echoed, a smile playing on his lips. "Is that what you call us?"

I shrugged, blushing. "Mei and I came up with it . . . for your, you know, your crew of friends." I bit my lip, meeting Asher's gaze. "Though I guess our crews have blended a little bit."

"They have," Asher said, stepping closer to me. My pulse spiked. "And I'm grateful to you for that."

"I'm grateful to you, too," I whispered back. "And I hope . . ." My blood was roaring in my ears, but I made myself say the words. "I hope you know I *do* feel the same way you do. Even if it also took me a little while to realize it."

There, in the middle of Flavorfest, Asher and I stood grinning at each other. My heart felt like it might burst.

"Just FYI," Asher said after a moment, "Mei's already booked you for a shopping trip and makeover between now and Valentine's Day. So she'll be devastated if you turn me down, and" — he swallowed — "she's not the only one. I know dances aren't really your thing, but I —"

"Yes," I interrupted. "I'd love to go to the dance with you." I paused. "But on one condition."

"What condition?" Asher asked, puzzled.

A wide smile broke across my face. "We have a pillow fight first."

So it was that on Valentine's Day, Asher and I stood in a teeming crowd of hundreds in Justin Herman Plaza with pillows at the ready, waiting for the stroke of six o'clock.

"I almost hate to do this," Asher said, grinning slyly. "You look so great tonight."

"Thanks," I said, blushing. "But if you don't use that pillow, I'll never forgive you."

Asher laughed. "You got it." He looked ridiculously handsome in a navy-blue suit and tie, his curly hair combed back.

I smiled at him and tightened my grip on my pillowcase, then glanced down at my own outfit.

Even I had to admit that Mei's makeover had worked a small miracle. The strapless burgundy dress she'd helped me pick out fit perfectly, and I'd grudgingly agreed to wear kitten-heeled black shoes that were really very cute. And for tonight, and tonight only, I'd let Mei and Mom blow my curls out into a long, sleek wave that waterfalled down my back. I'd even let Mei dab on a little blush and mascara. But I drew the line at lip gloss, remembering what had happened to her last year during the Great Pillow Fight.

Even though dresses and heels would never be my style, I thought that maybe I could get used to them every once in a while.

As the bell tower tolled six o'clock, I raised my pillowcase high over my head and brought it down on Asher's as he whacked his pillow into my back. We whaled on each other and everyone around us with our pillows, and soon, feathers were flying through the air like snow as people whooped and shrieked. I laughed uncontrollably as Asher pulled feathers out of his mouth, and thought that, no matter how old I got, I would never, ever outgrow the Great San Francisco Pillow Fight.

Half an hour later, it was all over, and Asher and I were dragging our pillow-decimated selves out of the feather-filled plaza toward the bench where Cleo and Gabe had been watching and waiting to take us to the dance. Though Cleo was fully recovered from her appendicitis, she had still decided to sit this year's fight out. She'd offered to be our chaperone instead.

Now, she and Gabe took one look at me and Asher, covered from head to toe in fluffy down softness, and busted out laughing.

"I can't believe I'm taking you to the dance looking like that," Cleo said as Gabe hailed a cab on Embarcadero to take us from downtown to Bayview.

I giggled. "Hey, if I can't go as myself, then what's the point?"

"Exactly," seconded Asher.

Of course, Mei was a little tougher to convince. When Asher and I walked into the Bayview school gym, I didn't have time to blink before Mei spotted me and nearly screamed in horror.

"My masterpiece . . . ruined," she shrieked, not even giving me a chance to respond before dragging me to the bathroom. But she'd brought along her makeup bag for just such an emergency, and in a matter of minutes, I left the bathroom in a freshly touched-up coat of glam, this time with a little lip gloss thrown on for good measure.

As we stepped back into the gym, Mei motioned toward the dance floor. "So," she said hesitantly, "what do you think of the decorations?"

I glanced around and smiled. I didn't know how she'd done it, but Mei had actually made the gym look like it was wearing one of her pink skirts. A sheer, blush-colored canopy draped gracefully from the ceiling, and ice-pink lights cascaded down from it, giving the room a rosy glow. The normally gray walls were covered in paper valentines of every size and shade of pink imaginable. Pink metallic heart balloons formed an arched gateway to the dance floor, and the snack table overflowed with cupcakes and chocolate-covered strawberries. The only thing in the entire room that *wasn't* pink was my contribution to the evening, a heaping platter of Bacon Me Crazy BLTs.

On any other day, I might've teased Mei about the explosion of pink. But instead, tonight, I hugged her and grinned. "It's the best *Mei*keover I've ever seen. I love it."

Mei beamed. "I'm so glad you do," she said, then gasped as a new song started playing. "Omigod. It's the Psychedelic Furs. 'Pretty in Pink'! How perfect!"

"I requested it just for you," Ben said to her, walking over with Asher. "I thought it could be our song," he said shyly, taking Mei's hand. "Let's dance."

Mei gazed at him dreamily, then gave me a smile over her shoulder as Ben whisked her onto the dance floor. Leo and Ann joined them, and I saw Tristan out there, too, spinning Karrie around the floor. He was twirling her so crazily that she was laughing in spite of herself. And for a second I saw a hint of a sweeter, kinder Karrie. We'd probably never end up friends, but I felt hopeful that we might not be enemies forever, either, and that was enough for now.

"So Mei and Ben have a song." I rolled my eyes at Asher. "Isn't that sort of . . . cheesy?"

Asher shrugged. "I don't know. I mean, you have a sandwich named after you."

"I do?" I blinked in surprise.

He nodded, looking proud of himself. "It's your Valentine's present. I just came up with it this week, and Cleo's adding it to the menu. The CounTessa. Bacon between two pieces of French toast smothered in habanero apricot jam. The perfect blend of sweetness and bite."

"The CounTessa," I repeated quietly, my heart thrilling. "I like the sound of that. It will fit in perfectly with the rest of the bacon menu."

Since Flavorfest, Cleo and Gabe had decided to give the Tasty Truck an all-bacon menu permanently. After all, bacon was what we were great at, and since we'd won the Flavorfest Best Award, bacon was what we were now famous for. We'd sold more BLTs in the last week than we'd sold over the entire last year, and if we kept it up, the Tasty Truck would be *the* destination for San Francisco bacon lovers.

Now Asher put his arm on the small of my back to lead me to the dance floor. "You know, I liked the goose-down look you had going on earlier, but I *love* this."

"Don't get your hopes up," I said as we started to dance. The feel of his arms around my waist made me wonderfully light-headed.

"It won't last. You'll just have to take me the way I am, bacon, bobby pins, and all."

"I love bobby pins, too," he said, touching the spot where a single rhinestone dragonfly bobby pin lay tucked in my hair. "Hey, there's only one tonight? What's it for?"

I laughed. "So I won't forget to tell you what a great time I had."

Asher's face fell ever so slightly. "Oh," he said, sounding disappointed, "I thought it might be there so you wouldn't forget to . . . kiss me?"

My heart gave a huge leap and butterflies filled my stomach. "I knew I could never forget *that*," I whispered.

Asher leaned toward me, and our lips met in a soft, lingering kiss. In my wildest dreams, I'd never imagined that I'd be at the Sweet Heart Ball, kissing Asher Rivers, who'd turned out to be the sweetest guy in the school.

Once upon a time, I'd thought that there could be nothing better than bacon. But I'd been wrong. This moment was definitely more delicious than anything in the world.

# Tessa's Recipes

A little bit of bacon makes anything better!
Tessa had fun cooking with it, and you can, too! Just
remember that bacon can get extremely hot while it's
cooking, or even when it's fresh from the skillet or
microwave. Always be sure to have an adult supervise
when you're handling freshly cooked bacon, and
whenever you're using a stovetop or oven. An adult
should also always supervise or be in charge of the
chopping and dicing of any ingredients.

# Bacon Me Crazy BLT

For the BLT:

>    2 slices multigrain or eight-grain bread, toasted
>    2–3 slices freshly cooked bacon
>    2–3 slices fresh or roasted tomatoes
>    2–3 leaves baby romaine lettuce, washed and dried
>    1–2 tbsp Tessa's special sauce

Cook bacon in a skillet over medium heat until browned and crispy. Remove from heat and set aside. Toast two slices of multigrain or eight-grain bread. Slice one fresh tomato. If you prefer roasted tomato, slice one fresh tomato, drizzle with olive oil and balsamic vinegar, and bake in the oven for 25 minutes at 450°. Tear two or three leaves of baby romaine in half and set aside. Put your bread slices on a plate and spread with 1–2 tbsp of Tessa's special sauce. Now, add bacon, sliced tomato, and lettuce. Enjoy!

For the special sauce:

>    1 avocado
>    ¼ tsp garlic salt
>    ½ cup sour cream
>    ¼ cup mayonnaise
>    1 tbsp lemon juice
>    1 tbsp Dijon mustard
>    1 tsp chipotle pepper
>    1 tsp crushed or finely chopped bacon

Mash one avocado with a fork or with a handheld mixer until it's a fine, creamy consistency. Add in garlic salt, sour cream, mayonnaise, lemon juice, Dijon mustard, and chipotle pepper. Blend well. Stir in crushed or finely chopped bacon. Spread the sauce on your BLT, and enjoy! Makes enough sauce for approximately ten BLTs.

# Bacon-Peanut-Butter Cookies

1¼ cups flour
¼ tsp baking soda
¼ tsp baking powder
⅛ tsp cinnamon
4–5 strips bacon, crumbled
4 tbsp butter, softened
½ cup peanut butter
½ cup granulated sugar
½ cup packed brown sugar
1 egg
1 tsp vanilla
½ cup semisweet chocolate chips (optional)
½ cup chopped honey-roasted peanuts (optional)
1 tbsp butter for greasing baking sheet

Preheat oven to 375°. Mix flour, baking soda, baking powder, and cinnamon in a large bowl. Cook the bacon in a skillet over medium heat until brown and crispy. Set on a plate to cool. Once cool, crumble bacon with your fingers. In a mixer, blend softened butter and peanut butter together. Slowly add in granulated sugar and brown sugar, mixing until creamy. Next add in egg and vanilla, mixing until fluffy. Slowly add dry ingredients, blending thoroughly. Stir in bacon, chocolate chips, or chopped nuts. Place scoops of dough onto a greased baking sheet and bake about 12–14 minutes, or until golden brown. Makes about a dozen cookies. Enjoy!

# Bacon-Bits Brownies

1 tbsp butter for greasing pan
½ cup flour
¼ tsp baking powder
¼ tsp salt
⅓ cup unsweetened cocoa powder
1 cup granulated sugar
1 tsp vanilla extract
½ cup vegetable oil
2 eggs
12 vanilla caramels
1 tbsp milk
4–5 strips bacon, chopped

Preheat oven to 350°. Grease 9x9 baking pan. Cook the bacon in a skillet over medium heat until brown and crispy. Set on a plate to cool. Once cool, crumble bacon with your fingers. Combine flour, baking powder, salt, and cocoa powder in a bowl and set aside. With a mixer, combine sugar, vanilla, and vegetable oil. Add eggs, beating until creamy. Gradually add in flour mixture until well blended. Pour into baking pan. Heat vanilla caramels and milk in a small saucepan over medium heat until melted, stirring constantly. Drizzle caramel sauce over brownie batter. Sprinkle with chopped bacon. Bake for 20–25 minutes, or until toothpick inserted into center comes out clean. Enjoy!

# Maple-Bacon Cupcakes

For the cupcakes:

    1¼ cups self-rising flour
    1 tsp baking soda
    ½ tsp baking powder
    ¼ cup finely chopped or minced bacon (4–5 strips)
    5 tbsp butter, softened
    5 tbsp brown sugar
    4 tbsp pure maple syrup
    1 egg
    ¼ cup milk

Preheat oven to 350°. Line cupcake tin with paper cupcake liners. Combine flour, baking soda, and baking powder in a bowl. Set aside. Cook bacon in a skillet over medium heat until brown and crispy. Set aside on a plate to cool. Once cool, finely chop or mince bacon. In a mixer, combine butter, brown sugar, and maple syrup. Add egg and blend. Gradually add in flour mixture and milk, alternating a little bit of flour mixture, then milk, until fully combined. Stir in the bacon. Pour batter into cupcake liners, filling each liner ¾ full. Bake for 18–22 minutes, or until a toothpick inserted into the center comes out clean. Makes approximately 8 cupcakes.

For the icing:

    3 strips of bacon, chopped
    1 8-oz package of cream cheese, softened
    2 tbsp butter, softened
    2 cups powdered sugar
    ⅛ tsp nutmeg
    2 tsp cinnamon
    ¼ cup maple syrup
    1 tbsp chocolate sprinkles (optional)

Cook bacon in a skillet over medium heat until brown and crispy. Set on a plate to cool. When cool, chop bacon. With a handheld mixer, blend cream cheese and butter. Gradually add in powdered sugar, nutmeg, cinnamon, and maple syrup. Blend until creamy and fluffy. Spread on cooled cupcakes, then top with additional chopped bacon and chocolate sprinkles. Enjoy!

# Find more reads you will love . . .

When you're stuck with the name Beauty, people expect beauty and grace and courage from you. And when you're a prince, you're supposed to be athletic and commanding and brave and tall. But when Beauty and Prince Riley's lives turn upside down, Beauty has to figure out just who she wants to be. And Prince Riley has to learn that even a beast's appearance can be deceiving.

Playing Cupid

Jenny Meyerhoff

**SCHOLASTIC**

wish

Clara Martinez knows what it takes to make a good match. So when her school assigns a project to create a business, Clara starts a matchmaking service for her classmates. But things get complicated when Clara starts receiving mysterious notes from a secret admirer. Despite being an expert for her friends, Clara is kind of clueless about her own love life. Can she gather the courage to fall in crush?

The Last Present

A Willow Falls book from the author of *11 Birthdays*

WENDY MASS

SCHOLASTIC

Amanda and Leo know something about birthday magic. When their friend's little sister, Grace, falls into a strange frozen state on her birthday, they'll have to travel in time to fix whatever's wrong. As they journey back to each of Grace's birthdays, they start seeing all sorts of patterns . . . which raise all sorts of questions. Amanda and Leo will have to travel much further than they ever imagined to save Grace.

# What's on your  list?